This is an unc⋯
Please v⋯
⋯

MW01595432

ABOUT TRIBUTE ACT

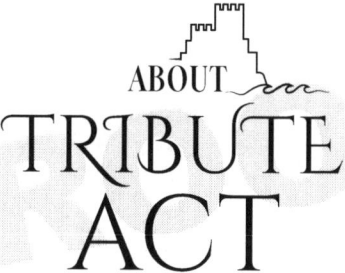

Nathan Bridges hadn't intended to settle down in his home town of Porthkennack—he just ended up staying after saving the family business from ruin. The truth is, Nathan can't stop himself from stepping in when problems arise. He's a fixer, the man everyone turns to. But even fixers can't solve everything.

When Nathan's sister needs an organ transplant, it's his stepbrother, Mack, who the family turns to as Rosie's only potential living donor. Nathan's curiosity about the stepbrother he's never met turns to shock when he realises that Mack is his latest—and hottest ever—one-night stand.

Nathan and Mack agree to forget their single night together, but that's easier said than done. When Mack moves in to Nathan's place to recuperate after surgery, it's not just the sexual tension between them that keeps growing. Against all the odds, and despite Mack's wariness of intimacy, the two men grow close enough that Nathan begins to wonder what it would take to mend the rift that's kept Mack and his father estranged for over a decade . . . and whether Mack might consider staying with Nathan in Porthkennack for good.

Riptide Publishing
PO Box 1537
Burnsville, NC 28714
www.riptidepublishing.com

This is a work of fiction. Names, characters, places, and incidents are either the product of the author's imagination or are used fictitiously. Any resemblance to actual persons living or dead, business establishments, events, or locales is entirely coincidental. All person(s) depicted on the cover are model(s) used for illustrative purposes only.

Tribute Act
Copyright © 2018 by Joanna Chambers

Cover art: G. D. Leigh, blackjazzdesign.com
Editors: Sarah Lyons, Carole-ann Galloway
Layout: L.C. Chase, lcchase.com/design.htm

All rights reserved. No part of this book may be reproduced or transmitted in any form or by any means, electronic or mechanical, including photocopying, recording, or by any information storage and retrieval system without the written permission of the publisher, and where permitted by law. Reviewers may quote brief passages in a review. To request permission and all other inquiries, contact Riptide Publishing at the mailing address above, at Riptidepublishing.com, or at marketing@riptidepublishing.com.

ISBN: 978-1-62649-684-2

First edition
January, 2018

Also available in ebook:
ISBN: 978-1-62649-683-5

a PORTHKENNACK
CONTEMPORARY

TRIBUTE ACT

Joanna Chambers

RIPTIDE
PUBLISHING

PROOF

Dedicated to all the fixers and donors out there.

PROOF

TABLE OF
CONTENTS

PROOF

ESSENTIAL
DISC NOTES BLOG

Christmas Stocking by The Sandy Coves spent thirteen weeks in the top forty in 1989, with four consecutive weeks at number two. Written by lead vocalist and guitarist Derek "Dex" MacKenzie, it was the band's only top twenty hit and remains a seasonal favourite. The single's success was helped along by a humorous video featuring Angie Ellis, a well-known soapstar at the time, but the comic touches in the video together with the upbeat fast-tempo production mask a pretty simple tune with surprisingly melancholy lyrics. Rumour has it Dex wrote the song about his failing marriage to Karen French. However, despite writing a song in which he begged Karen to stay with him, it was Dex who left the marriage—and the band after almost a decade together—walking out in 1990 for second wife and fellow musician Tammy Ferguson. He launched an unremarkable solo album, *Seashells*, a year later, but when his first and second singles both failed to break the top one hundred, he was dropped by his record label.

Bonus fact: After divorcing Tammy, Dex moved to Cornwall, married again and opened his own ice cream parlour. He never released another record.

PROOF

CHAPTER ONE

Do you remember last December?
We were so in love last year
I didn't have to try to please you
You were mine; I kept you near
Thinking now, I don't know how
We got in such a state, dear
Now we fight most every night
And losing you's become my biggest fear . . .
Christmas Stocking by The Sandy Coves, 1989

August

"I hope this doesn't make you late for your night out, Jonathan," Mum said.

Her voice was tight with anxiety, and though I couldn't see her from where I lay with my head wedged into the tiny space under the kitchen sink in Dilly's, I could picture her wringing her hands as she watched me work.

I didn't bother answering her, instead continuing to wrestle with the uncooperative plastic waste pipe. The plastic fittings should have come apart easily but were holding firm, and there was something *off* about the whole arrangement. I peered at it at it more closely.

It looked . . . crooked.

"Has Derek been messing about under here recently?" I called out.

"Not for a while," Mum replied. "Though come to think of it, the sink did block a couple of months ago and he had to clear out the u-bend. He might've had some bother getting it back on." She paused, then added, "In fact, now you mention it, I'm sure he said something about having to glue it back on?"

Fucking great.

Somehow, I managed to stop myself saying that aloud, though I couldn't suppress a long-suffering sigh.

I could see the problem now. Could see where Derek had forced the fitting too hard and broken it. The repair with . . . Jesus, what had he used? Superglue?

Derek, my stepdad, was a great guy to go to the pub with but he wasn't exactly the most thorough handyman in the world. A lick and a promise, that was his style. Which usually meant that Yours Truly would end up having to sort out the mess at some point. In fact, when it came to dealing with those sorts of problems—whether at Dilly's or at home—Derek tended to go for the easy way out. It was a bit of a bone of contention between us.

And one of the many joys of combining family and work.

I squirmed out from under the sink and clambered to my feet, opening my mouth to deliver a rant about Derek and his slapdash repairs—only to close it again when I saw how exhausted Mum was. She generally favoured a glam look, but it had been a long day and her make-up had all worn off. She had dark circles under her eyes too and, worst of all, her roots needed touching up. I frowned to think she'd done a shift today with her roots showing—she wouldn't even answer the door like that normally.

But of course, nothing was normal right now.

I sighed inwardly, glancing at the clock. It was already after five. She'd be worried about Rosie and anxious to get home, though probably feeling guilty about leaving me with this mess.

Or rather, bloody Derek's mess.

"Why don't you head off," I said gently. "You look exhausted. I'll sort this out and finish closing up. It won't take me long. And it's not far to Gav's."

Lies, lies, lies. It was going to take ages to deal with this and the drive was over an hour. I'd have to text Gav and warn him I'd be late.

"Are you sure?" The weary note of relief in her voice was

unmistakable.

"Yeah," I said. "I'll be half an hour tops here. You go home and put your feet up."

She gave me a tired smile and kissed my cheek. "Okay. Thanks, love."

Once she was gone and I'd locked up behind her, I texted Gav.

Mini crisis at café. Will be late. N x

His answer arrived a minute later.

No bailing, Nathan. You promised to come with.

I sighed, heavy, then texted back.

Not bailing - will get there soonest. N

The pipework under the sink was utterly fucked. It looked as though, after snapping one of the fittings in half, Derek had somehow forced it back into place and fixed it there with a mix of mastic and superglue, half of which had leaked inside the tube— No wonder it had blocked again so soon. By the time I'd worked out the broken part wasn't salvageable, driven to the nearest home store to pick up a replacement, driven back and fitted it properly, it was near enough eight.

I dragged myself out from under the sink, sweaty, tired and spattered with mastic and grime, and turned on the tap. When the water flowed down the plug hole I was ready to sob with relief.

"Back in business," I muttered. Thank Christ. The last thing we needed was to lose half our weekend trading with a plumbing crisis. And if I got a shift on, I just might make it to Plymouth for the long-awaited night out I'd been promising to my best friend for weeks now.

My stomach rumbled. A bacon buttie for breakfast had been my last proper meal and I'd been too busy for anything else all day. I'd found a Snickers bar in the glove compartment of the car on my way to the home store and had scarfed it down in about five seconds. And that had been it for food today.

I turned to the fridge, stomach cramping with hunger, and examined the contents. There were ingredients for heaps of things but I was too hungry to cook, or even assemble a half-decent sandwich, and anyway, the kitchen had been cleaned at the end of the shift. I didn't want to mess it up again. I scoured the shelves for something I could eat immediately. It was pretty much cake or nothing. Well, there was ice cream of course—Dilly's was, first and foremost an ice cream parlour—but in truth, you got a bit sick of ice cream when you worked with it every day. Instead, I reached for one of our best-sellers—the carrot cake.

Carrots were healthy, right? This would probably count as one of my five a day. Maybe even two if I had a big slice.

I thought about that, then served myself a double portion, added a sinful mound of whipped cream, and shoveled down the lot, eating so quickly I barely tasted it.

When I was done, I stared down at the empty plate unhappily. The cake sat in my stomach like a rock. I could practically feel my blood slowing in my veins, heavy with the fat and sugar I'd consumed.

When I'd lived in London, I'd had to work long hours, but I'd eaten better then than I did now. Which was shameful considering I worked in catering these days. London had so many healthy food places that it had been easy to follow a high protein, low carb diet, without having to plan much at all. Plus, having a gym in my building at work had meant I'd been able to work out most days. I'd been in way better shape back then than now. When I'd moved back to Cornwall I'd boasted to all my London friends about the relaxed and healthy lifestyle I'd be enjoying, but the truth was, I was more stressed now than I'd ever been and had put on— Well, quite a few pounds.

Sighing, I packed the rest of the cake back up and put it in the fridge, then took my plate to the now-unblocked sink and washed up. All I had to do before I left was stack the chairs on the tables and give the floor a quick once-over with the mop before setting the alarm, locking up and heading out.

Dilly's had a great location. Porthkennack was one of those cute little Cornish seasidey places tourists love. The café was on a narrow side street just off the sea-front. Even better, my place was only a few minutes' walk away, a second-floor flat in a cobbled lane up the hill with views of the sea.

My flat was small and cosy—though twice the size of my London place, with a spare bedroom for any friends who cared to visit—and I loved it. I loved living in the touristy part of town, despite how noisy it was, sometimes, on summer evenings. When I first came back to Porthkennack, it had been winter and almost unbearably quiet—I hadn't been able to sleep for the quiet after my years of living in London. It had been a relief when the first wave of tourists had arrived.

As I climbed the stairs to my flat, wearily rubbing at the aching back of my neck and yawning, I wondered if I could I face a night out tonight? Maybe a movie on Netflix and an early bed would be a better bet?

But no. As tempting as that was, I'd promised Gav that I wouldn't let him down again tonight. Especially since this was his first proper looking-to-get-laid night out since the big break-up with Carrie. And of course, there was the possibility of picking someone up myself—when I considered how long it had been since I'd had sex, I wanted to weep.

My trouble was, I'd never been into one-night stands. Ever since I'd met my first boyfriend at seventeen, I'd bounced from steady relationship to steady relationship. Currently I was in the longest dry spell I'd had since my teenage days, having broken up with my last boyfriend, Christian, shortly after moving back to Porthkennack. Preoccupied with sorting out the then-failing, now-recovering, family business, I hadn't had the energy for a long-distance relationship with Christian on top of everything else.

Perhaps that had been a clue—that I'd felt like I needed energy to keep it going. But honestly, it fit the pattern of how most of my relationships went—drifting into pleasant coupledom with a guy I liked, only to decide a couple of years later that I didn't feel strongly enough about him to make a permanent commitment. Maybe it was just how I was built—maybe I wasn't capable of more? That was certainly what Christian had thought. He'd said he wanted to be loved *"deeply and passionately"*—and he was right when he'd said I couldn't give him that.

I did like being in a relationship though. I liked companionship and sharing a life with someone. I liked having sex with someone who I knew inside out, and not having to wonder what that person thought of my body or whether they liked what I was doing. I liked being able to have unselfconscious, loud, joyful sex and I wasn't the kind of guy who found it easy to let go in that way with a stranger.

Whatever my reservations on one-night stands, though, I still felt like I *needed* sex. Though some of my relationships might have been emotionally lukewarm, they had all been physically successful. I loved sex and I was good at it. I was just atrocious at flirting. Too used to having a steady boyfriend and not having to make the effort to pull someone. It had made me complacent and awkward about the mating rituals of dating and hook-ups. The thought of approaching a hot guy in a club had me practically cringing. Well, at least until I imagined fucking said hot guy... And *that* thought was exactly the motivation I needed to get me moving towards my wardrobe.

I reached inside and pulled out my oldest, favourite jeans—threadbare, skin tight, and butter-soft—and a fitted black shirt that I figured I could still squeeze into, even after two slices of carrot cake.

And then I headed for the shower.

CHAPTER TWO

One of the downsides to living in Porthkennack was that the nearest decent gay club was over an hour away, in Plymouth. Luckily one of my best friends from my school days, Gav, lived there. What's more, he was bi, and, following the recent demise of his long-term relationship, he was desperate to get out and meet new people, of both sexes.

It was after ten when I finally arrived at Gav's. After he'd bitched at me for my lateness and forced me to down a couple of large vodkas to catch up with him, we headed out.

"I can't believe how nervous I am about this," Gav said as we walked. "My stomach's in knots."

"It's not that long since you've been clubbing. We went to Rainbow City at New Year's."

"Yeah, with Carrie. But do you realise it's been almost *six years* since I went to a club actually trying to meet someone? I don't know how to do stuff like that anymore!" He shook his head at himself.

"It's like riding a bike," I said, as though I didn't have exactly the same fears. "Besides, it's got to beat another night in watching TV."

Gav looked grim. "I suppose."

I bumped his shoulder with mine. "That's the spirit. You're not going to meet someone if you never go out."

He glanced at me, his expression disbelieving. "You're one to talk."

I sighed. "I know. It's been a while. The last time I hooked up was that night out at Rainbow City, and that's, what, eight months ago? God, I seriously need to fuck tonight."

Gav screwed up his nose. "Ugh. It's too weird hearing you talking about hooking up—you never used to do that."

"I never had the chance," I protested. "Five boyfriends over a decade with no time off for good behaviour. Then fuck all for nearly two years." I kicked at a stone with my foot, sending it skittering into the gutter.

"Yeah." Gav's sigh was sympathetic. "It's only been four months since Carrie moved out and I still feel like I've had an arm cut off. We were together for almost six years. I hardly stepped foot in a gay club in all that time, and even when I did, she was with me, so it wasn't like I was looking. Well, I was *looking*—we both were obviously—but we weren't *flirting*." He glared at the pavement. "And now I don't feel like I can do it anymore."

"If you're hinting that you'd prefer to go to a straight club, the answer is no way, my friend. I *need* to get some cock tonight."

He laughed weakly. "No, don't worry. It's not as if I'd find a straight club any easier. I can't remember how to flirt with guys *or* girls, Nath. I'm fucking bi-awkward."

I stretched out a hand and ruffled his pale hair. "It'll get easier," I said gently. "You just need to make the effort to come out—force yourself to meet new people. Practice."

"Aaaaand once again with the pot, kettle, black." He grinned at me and I laughed.

"I know, I know."

We turned the next corner, and there it was: Club Indigo. A couple of bouncers stood at the entrance, lording it over a thankfully modest queue. When they opened the door to let a few people in, a fat house beat leaked teasingly out.

Twenty minutes later, we finally got inside, paid a tenner to the cute twink at the desk, and headed for the bar.

"We need a drink," I told Gav, grabbing his hand and towing him after me. We were bloody freezing by then, Gav having insisted we leave our jackets at the flat, but we'd soon warm up, given how mobbed the place was.

Snaking through the dense crowd, we reached the bar and promptly ordered two Coronas and two tequila slammers. We did the shots, drained the beers, then ordered another round, snagging a little table with a couple of high stools when two other guys vacated it.

The drinks soon did their work on us, though in different ways.

It had been another long, tiring week for me and, although I had a little bit of a buzz going from the tequila, the last thing I felt like was dancing. This was the first time I'd relaxed in ages and I just wanted to kick back for a while and let the music wash over me.

Gav, of course, wanted to dance. He'd loved clubbing before he'd settled into coupledom with Carrie, and he couldn't tear his eyes from the mass of bodies writhing to the music. He tried to persuade me to join him, but I waved him off, knowing he'd soon find someone to dance with. I watched him disappear into the throng, white t-shirt glowing like a beacon under the UV lights, his shaggy blond surfer hair and pretty-boy face causing more than one head to turn.

After a couple of songs—and another beer for me—Gav reappeared, this time with a tall, built guy in tow. He had to be, what, six three? Four? Other than the height, he was an ordinary looking guy: light brown hair, nice enough face. Not quite in Gav's league though—not many people were.

"Introduce yourselves," Gav ordered. "I'll get the beers in." He scooted off.

The guy stared after Gav for a few moments before he finally turned to me. He seemed a little dazed. "Sorry." He held out his hand. "I'm Adam."

We shook. "Nathan," I told him, though I doubt he heard me. Already he was sneaking a glance in the direction Gav had gone.

"So," I said. "You just met Gav."

Adam was forced to give me his attention again. "Um—actually, no. We work in the same building—different companies but we sometimes end up in the same bar for Friday night beers."

God, Friday night beers. The office workers' weekly freedom call. I felt a stab of nostalgia for that TGIF feeling I used to get at the end of the week. It wasn't a feeling you ever got when you were running your own business.

"I didn't know Gav was bi," Adam added. "It was a surprise seeing him here."

"A good one?" I teased, lifting an eyebrow. Like I didn't know.

He laughed, then. "Very."

He had a nice laugh, and a genuine smile that turned his ordinary face into a much more handsome one. And God, he was into Gav—

as Gav approached us, beers in hand, Adam's stare became openly admiring, hiding nothing. Not the most mysterious guy in the world, this one.

While Gav set down the beers, Adam slid off his stool and tried to make Gav take it. They bickered flirtatiously about who should sit and who should stand and eventually both decided to stand, which was ridiculous given the height difference. I tuned their conversation out, content to sit back and relax. I had no desire to be a third wheel.

When Adam went to get another round of beers, Gav gave me an apologetic look. "Sorry, Nath, we're ignoring you, aren't we?"

I tipped the last of my beer into my mouth then set the empty bottle down and gave him a lazy smile. "Mate, I am *totally* fine. Honestly, it's good to see you enjoying yourself. And the truth is, having a few beers and taking it easy is just what I need. It's been quite a week."

"You sure?" he said. "I can ditch Adam if you want to go somewhere a bit more chill."

"I'm sure," I said firmly. "Go for it with this guy. Seriously. I'll be fine—I've got your spare key so I can head off any time I decide I've had enough. I'll text you if I bail."

He frowned. "I thought you wanted to hook up with someone?"

"Yeah, and I still might," I said, though the yawn that followed those words gave away my lack of enthusiasm. "Sorry. I'm so fucking beat."

"You've been working too hard," Gav said disapprovingly.

"Yup." I couldn't disagree. "Oh, look, here comes your boy."

After the next round of beers, Gav and Adam returned to the dancefloor while I slid off my stool and strolled back to the bar for what I'd already decided would be my last drink. I figured I'd stay another half hour, then text Gav. Maybe get a kebab on the way home. You usually got some salad in a kebab after all. Between that and the carrot cake, I'd be halfway to my five-a-day!

Most of the crowd were on the dance floor now, so the bar was much quieter. As I waited to be served, my gaze slid over the heaving throng of bodies. I couldn't even pick out any individual guys, much less pinpoint anyone I was attracted to. The crowd was like one big pulsing, breathing animal form.

I turned away, feeling oddly empty.

And that was when I saw him.

He was skirting the edge of the dancefloor, making a beeline for the bar. Most of the clubgoers were reasonably dressed up, but not this guy. Worn jeans, plaid shirt, scuffed-up boots and a beanie. Seriously, in the middle of a nightclub, a woollen beanie.

I didn't normally go for guys like this, but for some reason, I couldn't take my eyes off him. As he drew closer, he slid the beanie off and tucked it in his back pocket. His hair was dark—black maybe, or very dark brown. Difficult to tell in this light—and a startling contrast to his pale skin under the UV lights. He had a lean face with longish stubble, verging on an incipient beard. His eyes were what I really noticed though. I've always been a sucker for dark, soulful eyes and his were gorgeous, with a slight downward tilt at the outer edges.

When he was almost at the bar, he glanced at me and I flushed, embarrassed to be caught staring. He slowed though, meeting my gaze.

And smiled.

For a couple of beats, we just stared at each other, then he subtly shifted direction, joining me where I stood at the far end of the bar.

My mouth went dry and my heart began to pound with nerves and excitement.

"Hi," he said when he reached me. "Can I buy you a drink?"

"Um—okay."

So smooth. Fuck.

"What do you fancy?"

"A beer?" Why was asking him? More firmly, I added, "Corona."

He gestured for the barman's attention with a negligent lift of his chin I envied, especially when the barman immediately moved towards him, and with a smile he hadn't offered me all night.

I watched as my new friend gave the order, bantered lightly with the barman, and paid for our drinks. At last he turned back to me, handing me a cold, wet bottle of beer. He offered me the neck of his own bottle and I clinked mine against it in salute.

We drank then. I only sipped my beer but he took a long pull from his, his pale throat working as he swallowed.

My cock stirred.

When he set his bottle on the bar, I said, "Thanks for the beer. I'm

Nathan by the way."

He smiled. "I'm Mack. Pleased to meet you." Was that a Scottish accent?

I swallowed. "Likewise."

"So," he said easily. "Are you looking for some action tonight?"

Christ. There was direct, and then there was *direct*. Distantly, though, I heard myself say, "Yeah. How about you?"

Jesus, his *eyes*. I wondered if he actually felt sad right now, or if the impression of melancholy was just an accident of genetics—that slight tilt, and the dark, melting colour.

"Oh, definitely," he replied, a distinct smile in his voice. "Hopefully we're after the same thing—what exactly is it you want?"

I didn't know what to say to that. Did he want *specifics*? "Well, to blow off some steam, I suppose."

I was just playing for time with that one, but he smiled as though I'd pleased him. "Sounds like we're on the same page."

Are we?

He leaned towards me, and I thought he was going to kiss me right then. Disappointingly, though, he stilled before our lips touched and said, "Shall we . . . pay the bathroom a visit?" He raised an eyebrow in teasing enquiry.

God, I was into him, my cock stiff as a board at having him so near. Even so, my stomach knotted up at his suggestion. I wasn't into sex in club bathrooms. No matter how hot it sounded coming out Mack's mouth, I knew once we got there, I'd probably start hating it, feeling self-conscious and watched.

"No?" he said, at whatever he saw on my face.

I met his gaze. "Maybe somewhere—a bit more private? I'm not much of an exhibitionist."

He didn't seem to find that too absurd, just asked calmly, "Are you asking me back to your place?"

I made an apologetic face. "I'm staying with a friend tonight, and I think he's about to get lucky, which means I'll be on the living room floor . . ."

He seemed to think about that, gaze travelling over my face. At last he said. "Well, I'm at a hotel—we could go there if you don't mind a walk. It's on the outskirts of town though."

I swallowed against sudden nerves. Whispered, "Sounds good."

"Okay," he said, offering me a crooked a smile. Then he lifted his beer, drained it and set it on the bar. "I'm ready to go whenever you are."

PROOF

CHAPTER THREE

I found Gav and Adam on the dancefloor. They both had their T-shirts off already, Gav's smooth, wiry chest pressed up against Adam's broader, more heavily muscled one. Adam didn't look too pleased to see me, till he realised I was heading off—then his smile was huge. I pointed out Mack, who was standing at the doors waiting for me, and promised to text Gav the name of the hotel. Then I jogged back to Mack and we left.

We walked through town, across the busy centre, and out past the residential suburbs. We walked right out to the edge of town, into that odd no-man's-land of roundabouts, sliproads and industrial units that surround so many British towns. It wasn't a landscape for pedestrians out here. Pavements were dispensed with and the few drivers we saw stared at us curiously through their windscreens as we cut across grass verges and clambered over traffic furniture till we reached the big, soulless discount hotel where Mack was staying.

We walked through the tiny reception area, nodding a hello to the bored clerk at the desk, passing banks of vending machines stuffed with snacks, dead-looking sandwiches and toothbrushes on our way to the lifts.

"I'm on the fourth floor," Mack said as we entered the lift. It was only then I realised how little we'd spoken on the way out here. Mack had apparently been content to walk along in silence, and strangely enough, I hadn't felt the need to fill that silence, as I usually would with someone I didn't know. There was something oddly restful about Mack. He had a laid-back vibe that made him easy to be around.

Hearing his voice now, though, in the hushed silence of the hotel, brought me out of the comfortable daze I'd fallen into.

I glanced at him as the lift doors swished open and we exited onto the fourth floor. "Is that a hint of a Scottish accent I hear?"

"A bit of one," he confirmed, though his tone didn't exactly invite questions.

I followed him down a long snaking corridor to room 443, watching as he shoved the key card in the slot, then opened the door, stepping aside in an old-fashioned way to let me precede him. I felt slightly disconcerted by his manners, but walked past him as invited. The lights came on a moment later, the circuit completed by Mack inserting the key card into the slot by the door which closed slowly, heavily, with a quiet click of finality.

It was a surprisingly nice room for a budget place, dominated by a huge double bed. There was only a narrow strip of floor space around the bed, but who needed floor space with a bed that big? There was a decent bathroom too and a TV mounted high up on the wall.

A battered rucksack and a guitar case lay abandoned in the corner. Stuff had spilled out of the rucksack onto the floor, a scrambled heap of fabric and toiletries, like Mack had been rifling in there for something. The remains of his dinner—a fast food meal—littered a small table near the TV. The tea and coffee tray had already been ransacked, a little pile of tiny milk cartons torn open and upended on the table, two used teabags slumped against each other like tiny wet sacks. Mack crossed the room to flip on a lamp in the corner then killed the main lights. When we got to the stage of taking clothes off, I'd be glad of that.

Mack approached me, his expression watchful and serious. Really, he had ever such a nice face. Something in my chest twisted just looking at him.

He stepped up close to me, without touching. "So. What are you up for, Nathan?"

I met his gaze. "Whatever you like. Blowjobs, handjobs." I paused. "Fucking if you like—if you have condoms." I had my own condoms but I wanted to make it clear that wasn't negotiable.

Quirk of a smile. "I like . . . and I do. Do you have a preference for top or bottom?"

It was all a bit clinical, this sort of pre-negotiation, but necessary.

"I'd prefer to top," I said frankly. "It's not a deal-breaker though."

He smiled. "I can bottom."

His easy acceptance relaxed me. Sometimes I just really wanted to fuck. It didn't matter whether I was topping or bottoming—it wasn't about a need to penetrate or be penetrated. It felt more like, I don't know, a need to *immerse* myself. Get out of my own head.

I took hold of his hips and moved in for a kiss but he pulled back a little, evading my mouth.

I wasn't sure what to make of that. "Everything okay?"

He flashed a grin at me. "Fine, but let's get straight to the good stuff, yeah?"

I wanted to say that kissing *was* the good stuff but it was obvious he didn't agree and this sort of encounter called for compromise.

"Okay, sure," I said easily, mentally shoving my disappointment aside.

I reached for the buttons of his shirt and he didn't seem to object to that move. He watched as I worked them free, then pushed the soft flannel off his broad shoulders, revealing a plain white T-shirt that he quickly ripped off and tossed aside. His spare, lightly muscled torso was pale, his small, dusky nipples already hard. A trail of dark hair arrowed down his belly, disappearing into his jeans. My mouth watered. I wanted to hit Pause. Have him lie still while I licked him all over, but he was already wrestling with the buttons of his jeans, and it wasn't like I was going to complain. His urgency was fucking sexy, even though a part of me wished he would slow down and let me look at him properly.

He shoved his jeans and underwear down together, revealing more. Sharp hipbones, a nice, averagely-sized cock, hard and red-tipped with need. A dark nest of pubic hair and the long, lean legs of a distance runner.

He kicked his jeans away then peeled his socks off, sending them sailing over my head with a grin.

The whole strip took about ten seconds and he didn't so much as pause before reaching for the hem of my own shirt. A momentary panic seized me as I thought of his gaze on my own, far less lean body and I put my hand on his wrist, stopping him.

He blinked. "What's wrong?"

Immediately I let go. "Nothing." I forced a smile.

He studied my face for a moment, then gripped the hem of my shirt again, tugging upwards. I lifted my arms to help but with the shirt being such a close fit, I got caught up in it once it was over my head and couldn't see for a moment. It was probably only a second or two at most but with my eyes covered, I was suddenly horribly conscious of my undefended body, most especially the slight softness around my once hard belly. I wrenched hard at the shirt, faintly panicky.

When I finally wrestled it off and tossed it aside, it was to find Mack watching me, an amused twist to his lips. "Got a bit tangled up there, did you?"

I felt my face heat. "Yeah. I must have put some weight on since I bought that shirt."

Oh, fuck, no! *Why* did I say that?

Mack just grinned though. "Well, you look pretty good to me," he assured me and his eyes were so warm and appreciative that I couldn't help but return his smile, despite my self-consciousness.

I reached for him again, intent on kissing him, but he lowered his head, busying himself with unbuttoning my fly. "I'm dying to see what you've got in here," he told me as he began to push my jeans down, going to his knees in front of me.

Fuck, he looked good, kneeling naked on the thin hotel carpet. His shoulders were broad but he was rangy. It gave him a slightly ascetic appearance—as though he might be the sort of guy who might forget to eat occasionally, if he was busy with something else. Maybe playing that guitar. Not like me. I'm the prosaic sort that likes three square meals a day.

Mack eased my jeans down my legs. Mine didn't slide off quite as easily as his. While he was tall and slim, I was of a broader, stockier build, maybe an inch shorter and probably a good bit heavier. My mum used to call me *well-made* when I was an overweight teenager, which was a nice way of saying that I had a body type that ran to fat if I didn't watch my diet and exercise religiously.

But judging by Mack's reaction, he liked what he saw.

"Hmm," he murmured approvingly as he ran his hands up the back of my bare legs, giving his attention to my desperate thrusting cock. "Very nice."

He stuck out his tongue and lapped at my tip. I groaned, touching my hand to his shoulder to balance myself. Christ, it had been *so fucking long*. Mack glanced at up me, grinning, then set to, licking a stripe up the length of my cock then back down, right to my balls. He did it over and over, getting me wet and sloppy, and I moaned my pleasure—I've always been quite loud in bed and he seemed to like my noises, his enthusiasm rising in response to each reaction I gave him.

After a couple of minutes, I shifted my legs apart to give him better access and reached out to stroke his hair. When he pushed his head against my hand, I understood he liked it there and threaded my fingers into his dark, silky mop, loving the helpless groan of pleasure that simple gesture elicited. Easy to see that little gestures of subtle dominance aroused him, his licking motions becoming ever more ardent when I tugged gently at his hair.

So that's what you like, I thought. And I liked it too. I wasn't into spanking or anything but I'd always been a little bit on the toppy side.

After a while—and with a supreme effort—I pulled him off me, urging him to meet my gaze by tilting up his chin with my fingers. He blinked at me, glassy-eyed already.

"Can you take me deep?" I asked softly. "Right to the back of your throat?"

His eyes gleamed and he nodded.

"Okay then, show me what you can do." I loosened my grip, giving him his head and he dived back on to my cock, taking me all in one go, spluttering a little in his eagerness.

"Hey," I said softly. "Easy, okay? We're not in a hurry."

He nodded without glancing up and went down again, more slowly and smoothly this time.

It was hard to stay on my feet as he serviced me. The physical sensation of his mouth on my cock was amazing enough, but it was his eagerness that grabbed at me like a riptide. How he reacted to my words, to my touch.

His cock stuck out from his body, hard and dripping. He went to touch it but I tightened my grip in his hair and softly said, "Not yet."

He dropped his hand, moaning round my shaft, seeming to love being told what to do.

"Good boy," I said tenderly and he moaned.

I let him suck me another minute before I carefully pulled him off me. He strained a little to get back to my cock and I smiled, enjoying his ardour, and the ebb and flow of this strange new dynamic we were building between us, the hints we were each throwing out and responding to in turn.

I tugged his hair again, more firmly this time, and he stilled. "Come on," I coaxed. "Let's get you ready for my cock now, shall we? Get on the bed on your stomach."

He obeyed, clambering to his feet and climbing on to the bed, though he growled at me impatiently, "I don't need you to get me ready. You can fuck me now."

I ignored that. "Do you have some lube?"

He sighed, but answered me. "Wash bag near my rucksack."

I found the wash bag tumbled to the floor, its contents falling out onto the thin, rough carpet. I snagged the lube and a box of condoms and, on my way back to the bed, grabbed a hand towel from the folded stack on the shelf outside the bathroom.

Mack lay on his front on the white sheets. His arse was phenomenal. Firm, rounded buttocks with deep dimples at each side. I settled down beside him, stroking his back, his pale buttocks.

"Spread your legs," I murmured.

"I don't need any prep," he insisted, even as he obeyed. "Fuck me now. I want your cock."

"Trust me," I soothed. "You'll enjoy this. I'll have you so ready you'll be coming as soon as I get inside you."

He moaned at that promise and I smiled, drizzling lube over my fingers.

One thing about being a serial monogamist—you get really good in bed. Well, you can't beat regular practice at any activity, can you?

It wasn't just the sex I loved, though, it was the intimacy. And this—what I was about to do to Mack—was one of my favourite intimate things to do to my partners. To work them up, so slowly, so inexorably, that they'd be sobbing and begging to be fucked, riding my hand in desperation.

Somehow, I just knew this was exactly what Mack needed. The way he'd pressed his head against my hand as I stroked his hair. The way he so eagerly sucked me down, then told me he needed nothing. These clues pointed to a man who wasn't comfortable asking for things with words but his body was crying out for what he needed, silently begging me. For some reason, it felt like I could read him—and that maybe he could read me too. That maybe he knew how very much I liked my side of this.

I started slow, trailing my fingertips down his crack, easing his legs further apart before gently grazing his hole with my lubed fingers. Pressing a little harder, I rubbed at the taut ring, carefully slipping a single finger inside before topping up the lube. I added a second finger as I kissed his neck, his shoulder, and began to work his hole in earnest. My fingers dipped into him shallowly, then more deeply, until finally, I crooked my fingers inside him, brushing his prostate so that he just about came off the bed with pleasure. And through it all, he moaned and cried, hips helplessly jerking, a barrage of incoherent pleading on his tongue.

All of it so sweet to me.

"Look at you," I marvelled as he writhed beneath me, near sobbing. "Christ, you're gorgeous."

"Please—I can't—"

"Are you ready for me, Mack? I think you might be close now."

He babbled his agreement as I withdrew my fingers from his body, using the hand towel to wipe the lube from my hands before tossing it aside. "Turn over then."

He stilled. Then shook his head. "Let's do it like this."

I paused, disappointed, but there was no hint from him that he was willing to be pushed. Not on this.

"Okay. Can you get up onto your hands and knees?"

He complied, somewhat unsteadily, while I smoothed a condom over my painfully hard shaft.

I clambered behind him and looked down at him, all stretched and oiled and ready for me. Practically quivering with need.

Fuck.

I lined myself up and pressed forward. I'd prepared him so thoroughly that his body seemed to actually draw me in, welcoming me with a tight clasping heat that had me gasping at the sweet pleasure.

"Fuck," he gasped. "You were right, I'm going to come in about ten seconds."

I groan-laughed. "Me too."

We lasted a little longer than that, but not much. A few minutes at most. Mack came first, moments after I reached round and took hold of his cock. I'd intended to stroke him to completion but as soon as I circled my fingers about him, he started pulsing come, and after that, I had no hope. A few more thrusts and I was coming too, flooding the condom, my forehead pressed hard against his right shoulder.

We sank down onto the mattress together, slick with sweat and come.

Bliss suffused me. I was overcome with the desire to kiss him, but wasn't sure he'd allow it and wasn't brave enough to risk rejection.

After a minute, when I began to soften, I gently eased myself from his body, standing to dispose of the condom.

"Mind if I take a shower?".

He turned onto his back, sending me a lazy grin. He looked well-fucked and very pleased with himself. "Sure. Go ahead."

"Thanks," I said, a little disappointed when he made no move to join me.

When I emerged from the bathroom later, a towel wrapped round my waist, Mack was sitting up on the bed, seemingly unconcerned by his nudity.

"I don't normally invite hook ups to sleep over," he informed me, yawning. "But since you don't live here and your friend's taken someone home—and since this bed is huge—you can stay if you want."

It wasn't the most enthusiastic invitation I'd ever received to sleep over, but I was grateful for it. The last thing I felt like doing was trudging back to Gav's, to listen to him and Adam going at it all night. Besides, I found I was reluctant to leave Mack. "Thanks. I appreciate it."

I got into bed while he showered. By the time he came back through, I was just about dropping off.

"Sorry." I mumbled as he crawled in beside me. "I'm beat."

"Don't worry about it," he said gently. "Go to sleep. I need to anyway. I've got stuff on tomorrow."

Gratefully, I let my eyelids slide closed again and drifted off.

It was late—or rather in the very early hours—when he woke me. He was tossing around and mumbling, obviously upset. After a few moments, I realised he was dreaming.

At first I let him be, hoping he'd settle, but when he grew more distressed, I shook his shoulder.

"Hey—you okay?"

He came to slowly, in waves. First his voice quieted, then his body stilled. Eventually, he said, his tone weary, "Sorry. Nightmare."

"It's okay. Do you want"—I hesitated—"a hug?"

"No," he said quickly. "No, no, I'm fine."

"Okay."

We lay there, silent and awkward in the darkness. I felt strangely awake, hyper-aware of him lying beside me, still and unhappy. I could *sense* his unhappiness and it bothered me. I wasn't sure how I knew he was miserable but I did, I knew.

At last I couldn't stand it any longer. "Do you want to change your mind about that hug?"

"What?" He sounded so surprised I almost laughed.

"Why don't you let me hug you? It might make you feel better."

"Oh, for God's sake," he muttered, then almost crossly. "All right, fine. If you want to."

He was facing away from me and he started to turn, but I said, "Stay where you are."

He did as I asked and I snuggled myself up against him, my groin against his buttocks, my torso against his back. I tucked my legs up like his, spooning him, and draped my right arm over his side. Kissed his shoulder. A strange shudder ran through him.

For a little while he lay, stiff as a board in my arms, plainly uncomfortable. But gradually his body relaxed until finally, his breathing grew slow and steady and he was sleeping again, peacefully this time.

I must have fallen asleep soon after.

I woke just once more that night. I'd rolled away from him at some point and he was reaching out to me, touching my hip.

"Don't go," he whispered. "Hold me."

So I did.

PROOF

CHAPTER FOUR

It was hours later when I woke again. It was still dark and I was briefly confused as to my whereabouts. Then I remembered. I was in Mack's hotel and, discount or not, the giant bed was super-comfortable. I had fallen asleep in my usual position, lying on my left side, facing the door. I didn't have to turn over to know I was alone.

I could feel that I was alone.

Sure enough, when I sat up, the other side of the bed was empty.

The darkness was puzzling, since I was feeling incredibly well-rested. Leaning out of the bed, I hooked up my discarded jeans and fished around in the pockets for my phone, swiping clumsily at the screen.

10:09.

The fuck?

I glanced at the window. There was one line of bright sunshine where the curtains didn't quite meet in the middle. Black-out curtains.

Oh well, at least I wasn't due in for a shift in the cafe today. I did have some paperwork to clear up but that wouldn't take all day.

I got out of bed and headed to the bathroom where I took a long morning piss. I stared at my dick and thought about what I'd done with it last night. About Mack's face as I pushed my cock into his mouth. The way his body arched and writhed under me as I fucked him.

His words in the night between us.

"Hold me."

Had Mack had left, or had he just popped out for some reason and intended on coming back? And if he did come back, would he be up for another round of sex, time allowing? When did we have to leave the room anyway? Wasn't it usually 11:00 for checking out of hotels?

I slouched back into the bedroom, switching on the lights, and cast my gaze about the room. The rucksack and guitar case were gone.

Then I spotted the note.

Nathan,

Didn't want to wake you, sleeping beauty :-) but I've got to be somewhere today so I'm off. Room's paid—you've got to be out by 11.

Have a great life.

M

Short and to the point.

Nice note. Nice guy. Great sex.

The reason I felt so hollow? It had to be that serial-monogamist gene kicking in. The one that turned every guy I fucked into a potential boyfriend.

Yeah, that was it.

Gav picked me up at the hotel an hour later in my car. He'd brought all my stuff so I could drop him off then drive straight back to Porthkennack. We spent the journey back to his flat teasing each other about our respective hook-ups and how quickly we'd both ended up leaving Club Indigo.

"You going to see Adam again then?" I asked, waggling my eyebrows at him.

Gav grinned. "Well, I'd definitely fuck him again. My God, Nath, his *mouth*."

"Is that all? He seemed to be very into you. And a nice guy."

"He is a nice guy." Gav shrugged. "But I need to be single for a while. I can't just jump into another relationship like—" He flushed.

I understood immediately. "Oh. Like me, you mean?"

He sent me a brief apologetic look. "I only mean I don't want to end up in a rebound relationship."

"Hey!" I protested, "None of my boyfriends were rebound guys."

"No," Gav agreed. "You were never in love enough with any of them to *need* a rebound guy. The point is, you just sort of fell into every one of those relationships."

"What's that supposed to mean?" I said, offended. "I didn't fall into anything."

"Yeah, you did," Gav scoffed. "You'd let their eagerness to be your boyfriend carry you along for a while till you finally came to your senses and realised you weren't in love. And then you'd fall into exactly the same pattern with the next poor sap!"

"It wasn't like that!" I protested.

"So you loved them all, did you?"

"Of course I loved them—I still love them—all of them."

"You see?"

"What? No."

"You still love them now—all of them—the same as when you were with them. You were never *in* love with any of them. Not like I was with Carrie."

I opened my mouth to protest, then closed it again, frowning.

"Anyway," Gav said, waving an airy hand. "What about you and this Mack?"

"One nighter," I said firmly. "Didn't even get a number."

"Disappointed?"

I sighed. "Maybe a bit."

Maybe a lot.

"I thought you weren't looking for a relationship either?"

"I'm not."

"Then why . . .?" he trailed off invitingly.

I said, "There was just . . . something about him."

"Hold me."

I swallowed against a sudden lump in my throat, then before Gav could ask me any more questions, changed the subject, saying thickly, "Hey, keep an eye out for a coffee place will you? I need to get some caffeine before I head back to Porthkennack."

Thankfully, it was enough to distract him. "Fuck, yeah, coffee," he groaned. "I need a triple Americano right now."

And after that, Mack was forgotten.

By Gav, at least.

CHAPTER
FIVE

Chorus
I'll be hanging up my Christmas stocking
So, when Santa comes a-knocking
There will be a place for him
To put my Christmas presents in
But I don't need no fancy parcels
I don't want no bows or sparkles
All I want this Christmas Day
Is you telling me that you are gonna stay.
Christmas Stocking by The Sandy Coves, 1989

I had a *lot* of paperwork to deal with that afternoon, so the first thing I did when I got in the flat was make more coffee. Then I fired up the laptop, opened up Office and forced myself to start right away without even taking five minutes to check Facebook.

Dealing with the finances for Dilly's had been my first introduction to the family business, almost two years before. Mum was great in the café with the customers but she had absolutely no head for numbers. As for Derek, he was happiest in the kitchen. He made the ice cream and did some baking too, though most of our pastries and cakes were bought in.

Neither of them had been particularly vigilant with the finances. They'd let the books slide for years and it had come to a head over a big tax bill.

I'd been home the weekend Mum had her meltdown over it, or she mightn't even have told me. As it was, I'd asked to look at the books to see how bad things really were. Since my degree had been in marketing and business studies, I had a decent grasp of basic accounting.

I'd been shocked by what she'd handed over. There were no proper records, none of the invoices or receipts were properly filed, the tax records were a total disaster—they hadn't kept half the stuff they needed in case of an inspection—and when I checked the name of the company they'd set up in the company registers, I discovered it was about to be struck off for failing for file returns.

I told Mum I'd try to sort out the tax situation for them. I already had a demanding job in London but I'd figured I could spend a couple of months of my weekends sorting out the immediate mess and setting up new systems for them to follow, then once they were in place, I'd hand everything back to Mum and Derek and just check the books every once in a while.

Only the situation was worse than I'd imagined.

Much worse.

It turned out they'd borrowed against the house—Mum's house, the one my dad had signed over to her when they'd divorced—and sunk all the cash into the business. They'd given personal guarantees to the new lender too and were behind on their monthly payments. I hadn't realised things were so tight, but no one would have. Derek hadn't been living like a guy who needed to tighten the purse strings, had still been splashing the cash as much as he ever had. Only a few months before that, he'd taken Mum and Rosie to Florida and bought a new car.

It's not that he's a bad guy, but he's thoughtless. Feckless. When I was growing up, he was a great stepdad, fun and cool and easygoing. Never tried to replace my own dad in my life who I hero-worshipped, but yeah, involved in my life. Took his turn at driving me to swimming training at the crack of dawn and came to my football games. In fact, he was the first person in the family I told I was gay, and he was great about it. Took it in his stride and paved the way for me tell Mum.

But he can't run a business to save his life.

Luckily for him and Mum, just as everything had been going to shit for them, I'd inherited a chunk of money from my paternal grandmother. It was enough to bail them out, so that's what I offered to do. I paid off half the tax bill, negotiated a time-to-pay arrangement for the rest of it, cleared the loan against the house and got the personal guarantees discharged. In return, they gave me fifty per cent of the shares in the company. Of course, since the company had been worth basically nothing at that point in time, I hadn't really been getting anything beyond a piece of paper but I'd been okay with that. They'd needed the money more than I had right then.

I was ready to kiss my 'investment' goodbye forever after that, figuring that Derek and Mum would probably run Dilly's into the ground over the next ten years, but would get their living expenses out of it at least. But then, to my surprise, Mum asked me to join them in the business.

At first, I wasn't going to do it. My job in London was going well, and okay, I hadn't wanted to do that job forever, or to live the City lifestyle for much longer, but I hadn't been looking to make a change either. But then, one night on the phone, Mum confided that she was worried sick about my kid sister. Rosie had been depressed and anxious for weeks and though Mum had had her at the doctor a few times, she wasn't getting any better. She was convinced something was terribly wrong.

That had been when I'd realised how much everything had been getting on top of Mum: Rosie, the business, Derek's inability to stick to the new systems I'd put into place. So, on an impulse, I said I'd do it. Join the family business so Mum could cut her hours and spend more time with Rosie and stop worrying so much. I'd told myself that maybe I'd get the business on a good enough footing that my shares might actually be worth something one day.

My dad had been furious. He'd told me I was an idiot, squandering my inheritance then giving up a well-paid City career to become "an ice cream man". He was pissed-off at Mum for suggesting it to me in the first place and even more pissed-off at Derek for *not taking care of her* properly. And yeah, he was probably right, but like I'd told him at the time, I can't help how I'm wired. The bottom line is, I'm a fixer. When people—my family especially—ask for help, I can't say no. I'm a doer, you know? I make stuff that needs to get done *happen*. Right from being a kid, I did that. So of course, when Mum came to me about the Dilly's situation, I did what I always did.

I sorted it out.

When you're a fixer, people close to you get so they rely on you. It's not really their fault that they get used to you stepping in all the time, and assume that's going to always happen. But it makes it hard when something comes along that you *can't* help with. Something you desperately wish beyond anything you could do for someone but you . . . can't.

With the help of the coffee, I made good progress with the paperwork, blasting through everything in my pending file in five hours flat. All bills paid, all spreadsheets updated, all invoices and receipts and delivery notes checked and filed away, our nascent website updated and a bunch of emails sent out—two of them finalising details for meetings with local retailers. I'd been trying to arrange those meetings for a while, one with a big farm shop near Newport and one with Fletchers' Delis, a chain of four delicatessens in the South West. My big dream was to get Dilly's ice cream into the retail market. I planned to try selling through a few local places first, then, if we could get some traction with that, scale up manufacture before looking at pitching to a retailer with wider reach. Maybe even one of the smaller upscale supermarkets. It was a long-term project but it was important to me, allowing me to keep my marketing and business skills current.

At the moment, Derek and I were locked in a battle over which three or four flavours to launch from the thirty plus we offered at the cafe and how to package the product. Derek couldn't seem to see that we needed to differentiate ourselves from our competition, and that generic-looking vanilla and strawberry ice cream in bog-standard cartons wasn't going to cut it.

Since Derek and I couldn't agree on anything, I'd come up with the idea of hitting up a few local retailers for meetings. I figured we could ask for their expert advice and do a soft pitch at the same time— warm them up for taking some of our products once we were ready to go. Most people actually love giving out advice, provided you ask in the right way, so I'd thrown everything into my emails: a big dose of flattery, a slice of humble pie in the form of citing my youthful inexperience, and even a shameless celebrity pass—"*Our ice cream maker is my step-dad, Derek MacKenzie. He's an incredibly talented pastry chef and a bit of a local celebrity. (Remember the old festive hit*

My Christmas Stocking? *Derek is better known as Dex, the lead singer of The Sandy Coves! He's been known to burst into song over the ice cream machines . . .)*".

As I powered down the laptop, I called Derek to share the good news about the retailer meetings.

It was my little sister who answered.

"Hey," Rosie said flatly. "What's up"

"Just calling for a chat. How're you feeling today, Ro?"

"Like I always do—like shit. Do you want Mum?"

I was used to this now—her constant low-level anger and bitter resentment against the world and everyone in it—but I still found it hard to deal with. Before her illness, Rosie had been a bubbly kid. Maybe she'd have grown a bit grumpier anyway as she got further into her teens, but I felt it was mostly her illness making her so difficult. And really, who could blame her for being angry at the universe? Not me.

Patiently I said, "Is Derek there?"

"He's down the pub with Eric watching the match."

"Okay, put Mum on."

She clattered the phone down, yelling for Mum.

Mum picked up a minute later. "Jonathan love"—always my full name from Mum, everyone else called me Nathan—"are you coming for dinner? I'm making your favourite."

Shepherd's pie then. Shepherd's pie hadn't actually been my favourite meal since I was about twelve, but yeah, it was a more attractive option than cooking for myself tonight.

"Okay great. I'll come over now. I caught up on the books today and I've got some stuff to talk to Derek about anyway. Fletchers' Delis got back to me."

"That's good, you can tell us all your news when you get here." She didn't sound especially interested, but that was no surprise. She had other things on her mind these days what with Rosie being unwell.

I took a quick shower before I went over. There were still remnants of styling product in my hair from the night before since I hadn't washed my hair properly in the hotel this morning. I shampooed it twice and left it to dry on its own, not bothering to re-style my quiff, leaving the light brown strands to flop over my forehead.

As I brushed my teeth, I ran my hand over the bristle covering my chin and wondered for the millionth time if I should let a proper beard grow in. And with that stray thought, Mack from last night popped into my head. Not that he'd had a proper beard, but he'd had quite a few days' worth of stubble.

I'd liked his whiskers, the rasp of them on my skin.

I'd liked them a lot.

And why was I wasting time thinking about a guy I'd never see again?

Shaking my head, I reached for my jacket and headed out.

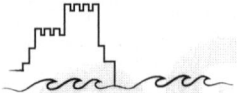

Mum and Derek's house wasn't far from my flat, just ten minutes' walk away in one of those tasteful new-build estates. Four bedrooms, en-suite, integral garage, that sort of thing. Not my cup of tea—I preferred Dad's traditional cottage a few miles up the coast—but Mum loved it.

As I walked over there, I thought about Rosie and how depressed and angry she'd sounded on the phone. I understood why—the poor kid was dealing with stuff no one her age should have to deal with—but it was difficult to know how to respond. We were all a lot more careful around her now, though somehow that only seemed to annoy her more.

Sometimes I wondered if she had a problem with me in particular. Because . . . well because I couldn't help her. She was used to leaning on me, used to me being the one in the family who fixed stuff, but now, for the first time in her life, I couldn't give her the one thing she really needed.

Mum's worry over Rosie's health had been well-founded. The doctor had thought she was suffering from depression at first, but when she'd started showing signs of jaundice and lack of co-ordination, further tests had led to a diagnosis of a rare condition: Wilson's disease. Her body had been accumulating copper for years and by the time she was diagnosed, her liver had already sustained serious damage. Damage so serious it couldn't be repaired. Now she was on the waiting list for a liver transplant.

When the doctors had told us it was possible to get a transplant from a live donor—a person could give away over half their liver and it would regrow to its original size within three months—we had all been sure that was the answer. Mum, Derek and I were all willing to donate, and family members were the most promising candidates. But in our case, it had turned out that not one of us was a match. And nor were any of the other more distant family members or friends who had been tested. So now our hopes were pinned on the donor list. And with every day that passed, it seemed like Rosie got a little worse, and we all got a little more desperate.

I'd been so certain that I'd be a match. As soon as Mum had first mentioned the possibility it had felt inevitable to me. It just made sense—Rosie and I were siblings, plus I was the right age and in good health. I didn't have a second's hesitation about going under the knife. The idea of giving up half my liver hadn't troubled me at all, even though I had a bit of a phobia about general anaesthetic. I'd have been able to deal with that to save my sister.

When they'd told me I wasn't a match, I'd been devastated. Worse, Rosie had been distraught. I'd taken one look at her face and known that, up to then, she'd been as convinced as I had that everything was going to be okay. After all, when hadn't her big brother been able to sort out any problem?

Well, her illusions had been well and truly shattered now.

The door of Mum's house was open as usual, and as soon as I stepped inside, the homely smell of shepherd's pie greeted me. I shucked my jacket and hung it up in the porch before wandering through to the living room. Derek was back from the pub. He was lounging on the sofa in front of the TV, beer in hand. He glanced up at my entrance and smiled. He had a great smile, did Derek. You could see how he'd ended up as front man of a band. It wasn't so much that he'd been particularly good-looking. He just had that elusive charisma people talk about. A glint in his eye that people responded to.

"I hope you're not hungover from your night out," he said. "Lorraine's made your favourite."

"I'm fine," I assured him. "Famished actually."

He chuckled and I walked past him to where Rosie sat, curled up in her favourite armchair, staring at her phone with her earbuds in.

She pulled the buds out as I approached, muttering an unenthusiastic "*Hey*". Her face had a yellowish sickly tinge I'd grown used to now. Between that and the bruise-dark circles under her eyes, she looked exhausted.

I dropped a kiss on the top of her head. Her hair—dark like Derek's rather than the light brown I'd inherited from Mum—smelled of apples. It was the same shampoo she'd always used, the one Mum used too, and for some reason, the smell of it made me suddenly sad.

"How you doing, kiddo?" I said.

She shrugged, eyes fixed on the screen of her phone. "Fine."

I suppressed a sigh at the monosyllabic response and turned back to Derek, dropping down onto the sofa beside him, Yawning, I asked, "What was the score on the Arsenal game?"

"One-nil."

I chuckled. "You'll be happy."

"Should've been at least three-nil but a win's a win. I'll take it."

I nodded at the TV. "What you watching?"

He made a face. "One of those singing competitions. Bloody awful. Is this what we've come to with music? This mediocre crap?"

On the screen, a young and very beautiful girl was toiling through a Whitney Houston song.

"She's a good singer," I pointed out, though I didn't disagree with him.

Derek snorted. "She's singing it to death. She doesn't even know what the song's about."

We watched her complete the final tortuous bars of the song to rapturous applause. When the camera flicked to the head judge, Derek cursed and switched off.

"Hey, it was just getting to the good bit!" That was Rosie. She glared at Derek.

"I'm not listening to that bloody idiot," Derek ranted. "What he knows about music could be written on a postage stamp with room to spare."

"He knows more than you do," Rosie muttered.

Derek's jaw tightened at that. "What, because he puts out mediocre records that sell to the idiots who watch this rubbish?"

"Uh . . . *yeah*," Rosie replied, voice dripping with sarcasm. "And he makes a shed load of money doing it, so I think he knows a *bit* about the business, Dad."

"Not everything's about money, Rosie." That was Mum. She'd emerged from the kitchen bearing a handful of cutlery and a bottle of brown sauce. She plonked it all down on the low coffee table in front of the sofa then came round to kiss my cheek.

"Jonathan, love," she said fondly. "It's good to see you. I like your hair like this." She was smiling but I could see how tired she was.

I shrugged. "It's the same as usual; it's just that I haven't put any styling stuff on it."

She ruffled my floppy fringe and laughed. "That's what I mean."

"Do you want a hand with dinner?" I made to get up but she pushed me back down.

"No, it's done. Wait here. Do you want a beer or a glass of wine? You'll need it after being at the books all day."

I smiled. "Some wine would be nice."

She headed back into the kitchen and I glanced at Rosie who immediately looked away, leaning towards the coffee table to snag the remote control.

I wished I knew what was going through her head. Was I imagining that she resented my inability to help her? Or was that how she really felt? It was so difficult to tell what she thought these days. She was so snarly all the damned time.

"How was school this week, Ro?" I asked as she began to scroll through the endless menu of channels.

"I didn't go in after Wednesday," she said flatly.

Mum came back in then, balancing three plates of shepherd's pie. "She wasn't feeling too good on Thursday," she told me, handing off the first plate to me. "So she decided to stay home."

She'd missed a lot of school lately. I wondered if she actually needed to, then felt bad for even having such a thought. Hardly surprising that school would be further down her agenda right now.

Rosie put on some mindless gameshow, turning up the volume high. Mum and Derek and I exchanged looks, but none of us said anything, though Derek glared at the television, probably only holding himself in check because Mum was there. Derek tended to let her call the shots on how to deal with Rosie

After dinner, Rosie disappeared upstairs with her phone while I told Derek and Mum about the retailer meetings I'd set up. When Derek repeated his belief in his vanilla-chocolate-strawberry strategy, I pointed out that the purpose of the meetings was to get some market intelligence on what actually sold. Unfortunately, that was the cue for Derek to get on his "*Do you know how long I've been selling ice-cream?*" soapbox. Again.

When things started getting tetchy, as they inevitably did, Mum—ever the placator—interrupted to brightly suggest we put a film on. She called Rosie down, demanding she help choose. They eventually settled on some shitty middle-of-the-road romcom. It was deeply awful, but since I was beat, and since Leonard, Mum's pure white Persian, had settled himself on my lap, I let my eyes drift closed and slipped into a doze.

It was the doorbell that woke me some time later. I lurched back to wakefulness with the chimes ringing in my ears. The credits were rolling on the TV screen and Mum and Derek were looking puzzled.

"Are we expecting anyone?" Derek asked, though he made no move to get up.

"No." Mum set her wine glass on the table and got to her feet. "I suppose it could be Val though."

As she went to answer the door, I glanced at my watch. It was just past nine—not the usual time for someone to pop by at the weekend.

Derek reached for the remote control and turned the volume down on the TV.

"Hey!" Rosie protested.

"*Shhh,*" Derek said, listening to the muffled voices. I listened too, but all I could hear was the vague rumbling of speech, Mum's distinctive Cornish accent and another one. Male. Deeper, quieter.

At length the front door closed. When Mum walked back into the living room, I expected her to be alone, but she had someone with her.

Someone I recognised.

Mack.

I opened my mouth to say his name, but before I could do so, Derek stood up, his movements curiously jerky.

"Dylan—" he gasped,

Dylan?

Mack's gaze—wide-eyed and faintly panicky—flitted between us all. For a moment it rested on me, and it seemed as though there was an unspoken plea there, in the dark, liquid depths.

Then he looked at Derek.

"Hi, Dad. I came as soon as I got your letter."

CHAPTER SIX

Mum was crying.

She was crying and holding Mack's hand. Mack looked deeply uncomfortable with the contact, but to his credit, he didn't pull away. Twice our eyes met and twice he dropped his gaze. Neither of us mentioned the previous night.

I'd been nine when Derek and Mum had first got together. I remembered him going up to Scotland occasionally back then to see his own son. Even after Mum and Derek had got married, they used to talk about Dylan coming down to visit over the summer holidays at some point. Derek had kept saying how the two of us could be friends and I could take him down to the beach with me. Show him round Porthkennack.

I'd had a secret fascination with this other boy, just a year younger than me. I used to make elaborate plans of how I'd entertain him when he came to visit. But he never did come, and as time passed, it seemed like Derek mentioned him less and less. Then, one evening—we'd been sitting round the TV, eating dinner—I'd asked, with all the diplomacy of a self-absorbed teenager, whether Dylan was *ever* going to visit us.

Derek had got this funny look on his face and I'd realised I'd put my foot in it. I'd thought maybe he was going to get angry with me, but he hadn't. He'd just got up very quietly and left the room. And when I'd tried to ask Mum about it, she wouldn't explain.

It was years later that she'd told me, one night after too many glasses of wine, that Derek and Dylan had argued on one of Derek's visits and Dylan had told him he didn't want to see him again. Derek had taken him at his word and Mum had been unable to persuade Derek to go and sort things out with him.

I'd been shocked. My easy-going stepdad, the guy who drove me around and took me to football and swimming training and nagged me to do my homework, had argued with his own son badly enough that they hadn't seen each other since?

Given the state of their relationship, I'd stopped expecting to ever meet Derek's son. It had been easy to forget he even existed—Derek hadn't mentioned him in years.

But now here he was.

Dylan.

Mack.

Sitting on the sofa next to my Mum as she clutched his hand with one of hers and wiped away her tears with the other.

"I'm s—sorry," she hiccoughed. "You must think I've gone mad. Only, it's so good to finally meet you, Dylan love."

Derek was standing awkwardly by the mantelpiece, his body language screeching his discomfort and adding to the strained atmosphere—certainly Mack kept sending him wary sidelong glances. Rosie sat curled up in her usual spot, silent but watchful, her eyes all but eating up this new half-brother who had suddenly presented himself.

Mack offered Mum a tight smile and said, "It's good to meet you too. I'm sorry it took me so long to get here, but I only got the letter a few days ago."

"Letter?" Mum glanced at Derek, her eyes welling up. "I thought you didn't know where he was?"

"I didn't." Christ, Derek looked awful: miserable and uncomfortable and somehow shell-shocked. "I didn't want to get your hopes up."

Mack cleared his throat. "He sent it to my grandparents so it took a while for the letter to reach me. I don't see much of them—I only speak to them every now and then."

Mum pressed her lips together and blinked hard, trying to keep back another flood of tears. "I'm sorry," she whispered. "It's awful that we didn't even know where you were living."

She glanced at Derek again and he stared back, ashen-faced. Mack himself was expressionless, though there were tell-tale signs of discomfort. His jaw was clenched tight, and his throat bobbed nervously. My gut twisted in sympathy.

Mum took a deep breath and turned her attention back to Mack. "So, where do you live now?"

He shrugged. "I move around a lot. I've been in Manchester for the last few months, but the bar where I've been working is closing for renovation so I was thinking of heading back down to Essex. Or maybe London."

Mum nodded but her eyes looked suspiciously shiny and I knew why. She had a big thing about family and home, and hearing that Mack—her own stepson—didn't seem to have that would be eating her up.

Fuck, I thought, *please don't start crying again. It's obvious he hates it.*

"Anyway," he went on. "Like I said—I got Dad's letter a couple of days ago. It'd been at my gran's for a few months but I only found out when I called her a couple of weeks ago and she forwarded it to me. And . . . well, here I am."

"Why didn't you call me first?" Derek asked, almost desperately. "I put my number in the letter. I *asked* you to ring me."

"Derek!" Mum hissed. "He's come all this way!"

"I know," Derek said, flushing. "All I mean is it would've have been better if we could have spoken first. It wouldn't have been such a—you know, such a shock."

Another shrug from Mack—that seemed to be something he did a lot. A speaking gesture that I was beginning to interpret as *It doesn't matter.*

"I was going to call," he told Derek. "But every time I dialled the number, I ended up disconnecting before you could answer. I just . . . I dunno, I felt weird speaking to you after so long, especially after the last time. And doing it by phone?" He shook his head in swift rejection of that idea. "In the end, I decided to get on a bus so we could at least talk face to face."

"When did you get here?" Mum asked and Mack's gaze flicked briefly to me, making my stomach flutter, before he quickly looked away again.

"I only got to Porthkennack earlier today. I came over this afternoon actually, but no one was in, so I thought I'd come back later.

Leave it late enough to make sure you'd be at home this time."

Mum patted his hand and said warmly, "Well, we're really glad you came, aren't we, Derek?"

"Yes, of course. Listen, Dylan—" But before Derek could go on, Mack was speaking over him.

"Dad—let's cut to the chase here, okay? You wrote to me for a reason. You wanted to know if I could help Rosie." He glanced at Rosie here, offering her a small smile. She stared back, wary and fearful, like she was scared to hope.

"We're the same blood group, you and I," he told her. "According to Dad, that means I might be able to donate some of my liver to you." He paused, adding more softly. "And if I can, I will."

Rosie covered her mouth with her hand. A moment later, a sob broke out of her, a pained, raw sound that made my throat ache. Mum started crying again too, while Derek covered his face with his hands.

Mack glanced around, plainly uncomfortable with all the emotion, and the death-grip Mum still had on his hand. I caught his eye and gave him a nod, mouthing *Thank you* at him, before going to Rosie, lifting her up right out of her chair—even at fifteen she was small and light as a child—and sitting back down with her in my lap while she sobbed her relief into my shoulder.

I wasn't sure if my attempt at reassurance had helped Mack at all, but he didn't get up, or try to leave, which was something. He sat quietly while Mum composed herself and found her voice again.

"Dylan, love, you...you can't imagine what this means to us—we'll never be able to thank you." She drew in a long, quivery breath. "Of course, you'll have to be tested before we can know for sure whether you can be a donor but we can get that arranged straightaway."

Mack nodded. "Yeah. I understand." He glanced at Derek, who stood watching, tense and tight-lipped, then at Rosie, whose sobs were quieting as I rubbed slow, comforting circles on her back.

Derek cleared his throat then. "Dylan, listen, I *am* glad you came. I just"—he broke off, seeming lost as to what to say—"I just wasn't sure what you'd make of my letter, and I've wanted to get back in touch for so long—"

Abruptly, Mack tugged his hand free from Mum's grasp and stood up, facing his dad. "Can we not do this? I'm not here for a reunion,

Dad. I'm just here to help my sister, if I can. That's all."

He didn't say it harshly—if anything, he sounded desperate—but Derek went white and fell silent. Mack immediately turned his attention back to Mum and it occurred to me that, despite how emotional she was, she was probably the easiest one of us for him to cope with. He plainly didn't want to speak to Derek and didn't seem to know what to make of Rosie. As for me, well, having me in the room probably wasn't making things any easier. Not if he felt as unbalanced as I did by seeing him again.

"Look, this is a lot for me to take in," Mack said, rubbing the back of his neck. "And not just me—all of us. Why don't we all sleep on it, yeah? I'll come back tomorrow and we can talk about the arrangements for me to get tested."

Mum got to her feet slowly. "You're going?" she said, her dismay palpable. "But—aren't you staying with us?"

Mack shook his head. "I've got a B&B."

"Oh, but there's no need for that," Mum protested. "We've got a spare room."

"Um—no offence," Mack said, taking a step backwards, "but I kind of need some space right now. You probably do too."

"Okay," Mum said reluctantly. "Whatever you're comfortable with, love. But maybe we could have your number? I'll write down ours for you." She scurried off to fetch paper and a pen and was soon back with a list of numbers. "That's the landline," she said, pointing to the top one, as though Mack wouldn't be able to tell a landline from a mobile number. "Plus mine and Derek's mobiles. And Jonathan's too. If you can't get hold of either of us, call Jonathan. He always knows where we are—better than we do ourselves usually!" She gave a strained laugh and looked at me. "Isn't that right, love?"

"Jonathan," Mack repeated and glanced at me.

"Most people call me Nathan," I explained, my gaze firm on him. "Mum's the only one who insists on calling me by my Sunday name."

He nodded, meeting my eyes. "Most people call me Mack."

I didn't know if that exchange meant anything to Mack, but to me, it meant something. It meant that the honesty I'd felt between us last night hadn't been fake. And somehow, it settled me, knowing that. That *Dylan* was still *Mack*.

In that moment, I knew he'd always be Mack to me.

Mack dropped his gaze first, tucking the list of numbers into his pocket and rattling his own number off for Mum.

"So," he said, once she had it down, "I'll head off now. Give you some peace."

Mum grimaced at that remark, though she managed to salvage a weak smile at the last moment. "I'll give you a lift to your B&B if you like, love, which one is it?"

"You don't need to do that," Mack said quickly. "It's just ten minutes from here on the sea front, and I could do with the fresh air, to be honest."

"Okay," Mum said. She was wearing her brave face but she was plainly anxious and I knew why. She was worried Mack was going to go back to his B&B and change his mind. Decide he wasn't minded to help his estranged dad's other family after all. And really, why should he? What had Derek ever done for him? What had any of us?

Gently, I shifted, murmuring in Rosie's ear, "I need to take care of something for Mum, okay?" She nodded and stood, letting me up, her gaze fixed on Mack.

"I'll walk you down to your B&B," I told Mack. "I'm heading off now too anyway."

Mum glanced me, her gaze relieved. "That's a good idea, love," she approved, clearly liking the idea of at least knowing where Mack was staying. Mack was less easy to read, his only reaction a brief nod.

We headed out into the hall to fetch our jackets, Mum talking Mack's ear off about the next day's arrangements. She finally, reluctantly, let us go a few minutes later. As we called our goodnights to each other, she stood there, framed in the light of the doorway, a fragile, hopeful figure.

"I didn't know who you were," Mack said, as we strolled towards the sea-front. He didn't seem to object to me walking with him, which was a relief.

"I figured," I said. "Same here."

"It's kinda weird."

I glanced at him. "How so?"

He met my gaze just as we passed under a streetlight. Those eyes. So dark and melty. Making my stomach turn over with helpless lust.

"Technically, we're step-brothers."

I gave a strained laugh. "Right, I see what you mean. But it's not like we met before we hooked-up."

"True," he murmured, looking away, keeping his gaze fixed forward.

An awkward silence grew between us. I searched my mind for something innocuous to say to break it, but found myself blurting out, "Why did you leave the hotel without waking me this morning?"

His gaze met mine again. Carefully he said, "You said you only wanted to blow off some steam."

"Yeah," I agreed. "Even so. You could've, you know, said goodbye."

He shrugged. *It doesn't matter.*

But it mattered to me.

At last he said, "Don't get me wrong, last night was great, but I knew I was coming here today, and that afterwards, I'd either be heading straight back to Manchester or going into hospital to have half my liver cut out. I wasn't in the market for anything more than a hook up."

It was a fair point, but I still felt faintly hurt. Despite what I'd said to him, it hadn't felt like a casual fuck to me.

I sighed and shoved my hands deeper into my pockets, saying nothing, and for a while, we walked along in silence.

When we turned off Cockle Lane onto the seafront, it occurred to me that we were getting close to his B&B—and that I wasn't quite ready for this to end.

Whatever *this* was.

Before I could think better of it, I blurted out, "Do you want to get a beer?"

He turned to look at me and his expression was wary—wary but with a hint of interest. I added softly. "Just to talk. It's been a hell of an evening."

He rubbed the back of his neck. It was an oddly vulnerable gesture—another one I already recognised from him. It was the weirdest thing, but seeing him do that made me want to step right up to him and wrap my arms round him. Give him a reassuring hug.

Instead, I waited.

Honestly, I expected rejection. Another *I need some space*, but when he finally spoke he said, "Yeah okay, why not. One beer can't hurt."

CHAPTER SEVEN

On reflection, the Sea Bell probably wasn't the best place to take Mack. I was so used to the place, I'd forgotten how unwelcoming it could be to newcomers. A dozen heads turned when we entered, and whilst I got the usual grunts and nods, Mack garnered assessing stares, even though he was with me.

Not that he seemed too troubled.

"There be a stranger in town," he murmured in a comedy Cornish accent as we headed for one of the tiny tables.

I grinned. "Yeah, it is a bit like that. Sorry."

Mack shrugged, though this time with a hint of smile playing at the corner of his mouth.

"What do you fancy?" I asked as I hooked my jacket over the back of wooden chair. "Pint of the local brew?"

"What's that then?"

"Chough's Nest."

He looked dubious. "I think I'll just take a pint of lager, thanks."

"Coward," I chuckled. "Okay, gimme a minute."

Jago was already pulling my pint when I reached the bar. "Who's your friend then?" he asked darkly, eyes narrowed with suspicion.

"Evening, Nathan, what can I get you?" I replied cheerfully.

"I'm already getting yours," Jago pointed out. "So who is he?"

"Um . . . family friend," I improvised. "And he's having a pint of lager, thanks."

Jago huffed, a sound that somehow managed to convey agreement and contempt in one. "Is he from round here then?"

I shook my head. The accent would give Mack away soon enough so I added briefly, "Scotland."

"Oh right. One of Derek's side, is he?"

"Yeah," I said, my tone vague. "You got anyone playing tonight?"

The Sea Bell held a proper folk night every Saturday but a lot of musicians hung out there who might play a few songs ad hoc, if they were in the mood.

"Andy's in," Jago said tipping his head at a scruffy bloke at the end of the bar, greying hair held back in a ponytail. "He might get his guitar out later, I s'pose."

I didn't much care, but it seemed to have worked as a change of subject. Jago put the two pints up on the bar and I paid, then headed back to the table where Mack waited.

As I approached him, I wondered what it was about Mack that struck me as odd. It was only as I reached the table that I realised—he wasn't fiddling with a phone like most people did when they were left on their own in a pub. He was just sitting there quiet, thinking.

"One pint of pissy, generic lager," I said, setting his glass down in front of him. I sat down opposite, lifting my own glass to my lips to take a swig, giving an appreciative sigh after. "And one pint of fine, locally-brewed Cornish ale."

"Yeah, well, I'll stick with the pissy lager, thanks," Mack replied dryly. "At least I've got a fair idea what's in it."

He took a drink and I watched him, reminded, inevitably, of the night before when he'd stood opposite me in Club Indigo, tipping up his beer bottle, slim throat bobbing as he swallowed, dark gaze full of promise.

It wasn't full of promise now. More wary.

"So," I said. "It's been quite a day for you."

He gave a dry laugh. "You could say that." Then he sighed. "I should have called first. It wasn't cool, turning up without warning."

I felt oddly aggrieved on his behalf. "Hey, he's your dad. You get to turn up whenever you like."

"Yeah? Try telling him that. He was horrified." He shook his head and even offered a lopsided smile, but I could sense he was hurt, and I hated it.

I remembered Derek's expression earlier as he'd berated Mack for not calling first and honestly, right then, I could cheerfully have punched my stepdad. But surely he hadn't really been horrified to see

Mack? Surely it was shock that made him react like that?

I let a moment pass then said gently, "He was surprised, for sure, but of course he wants to see you—he wrote to you, didn't he?"

Mack's look was wry. "He wrote to me because he wants me to donate my liver to my little sister." He lifted his lager and took another swig. Set it down. "And that's fine. It's not like I'd've come for any other reason. Like I said back there, I'm not interested in some big reunion. It's way too late for that."

My heart twisted painfully in my chest at those words. I didn't know what to say. What could *I* say after all? I was the guy with *two* dads—one of them his. What did I know?

"Speaking of which," Mack continued, frowning at his pint of lager. "I shouldn't be drinking any more booze. In case I'm a match." He pushed it a couple of inches away.

I couldn't help thinking about him last night, reaching out to me in the dark. His words.

"Hold me."

He had needed me last night—or at least, he'd needed someone. We all needed someone, sometimes. And God help me, but I'm a fixer.

I began, my tone tentative, "Maybe Derek—"

His hand landed on my forearm, warm and firm. "Don't, okay? I don't want to talk about my dad." He gave a half-smile to take away the sting and I nodded.

Just then, an electronic feedback shriek made us both jump.

"Sorry!" a guy yelled out—it was the pony-tailed guy from the bar, plugging his guitar into a speaker at the tiny stage area. Andy, Jago had called him.

"Looks like we're getting some music." Mack seemed pleased, watching the guy set up his equipment with obvious interest.

"You're a musician, aren't you?" I said.

He turned back to me, eyebrows pleated over the bridge of his nose. "Yeah, kind of. How did you know?"

"You had a guitar case in your hotel room."

"Oh, right." He shrugged. "I suppose, it depends on your definition of musician. I play, but mainly for myself, not to make a living. It's not like I'm hoping to hit the big time."

"You're not a professional then?"

"Nah, I just love to play. As soon as you start trying to make money or get known, that gets tainted, you know?"

Tainted. Interesting choice of word

"So what do you do the rest of the time?" I asked.

"All sorts. I was working as a barman in Manchester till last week but I've been a kitchen hand, waiter, labourer, cleaner, worked in warehouses and factories." He offered me a small smile. "I'll turn my hand to pretty much anything. What about you?"

I sipped my pint. "I studied marketing and business studies at uni. Worked in London for a while, then a couple of years ago, I came back to Porthkennack."

He gave me a curious look. "Why?"

It hadn't occurred to me he wouldn't already know but of course he didn't.

"I—um—I work in the family business. Dilly's."

"Dilly's? Wait"—he frowned, thinking—"Do you mean the ice cream shop my dad bought down here?"

I shifted awkwardly. "Yeah. That's it. It's more of a café now though. We still make and sell ice cream but we do breakfasts, lunches and afternoon teas. We're hoping to expand into next door at some point." I realised I was babbling and stopped talking abruptly.

Mack eyed me for a long moment, his expression unreadable. Impossible to ignore the obvious fact that this might prove to be a source of resentment between us. Me, the stepson, working with Mack's dad in the "family business", while Mack scraped by in what sounded like a series of temporary jobs. But in the end, all he said was, "You gave up a fancy career in London to sell ninety-nines in Cornwall?" To my relief, he chuckled. "You must be mad."

I laughed too. "I do make the odd ninety-nine," I admitted, "But my main role is dealing with all the business stuff—the boring stuff. Derek makes the ice cream, Mum and me run the cafe between us and we have a couple of part-timers to help out."

Mack raised a brow. "Must be demanding."

I glanced at him, wondering if there was any sarcasm there, but it didn't seem like it. "It can be," I said lightly.

Over at the stage area, Ponytail Andy hopped up onto a tall stool and began playing a few exploratory chords. Mack watched him intently. After a few moments he said, without looking at me, "What happens if I'm not a match?"

"Rosie stays on the waiting list," I said. "And we wait to see if a donor comes up. It could happen."

He nodded, tight-lipped.

"Fingers crossed you'll be a match though," I added.

"Yeah," he said softly. "Fingers crossed."

We stayed for Andy's short set—he played four songs, only one of which I recognised, an early Bob Dylan hit. He was a good guitarist but an indifferent singer and I pretty much zoned out while he was playing. Mack listened attentively though.

A couple of times, Mack reached for his pint, only to remember his decision not to drink it, and withdrew his hand. After a bit, I got up, taking the pint away, replacing it with a Coke. Mack blinked at me when I set the fresh drink down.

"Thanks." He sounded surprised.

Our drinks were long finished by the time Andy started packing up.

"Do you want another?" I asked, gesturing at Mack's empty glass.

He yawned. "Nah, I think I'll head back to the B&B now."

I was tired myself, but still, I felt oddly disappointed at the thought of the night coming to an end, though I hid my thoughts behind an easy smile, reaching for my jacket.

"Actually, can you wait a sec?" Mack said quickly. "I'll only be a minute."

I subsided back into my chair. "Sure."

He darted off to the stage area where Ponytail Andy greeted him with a friendly smile. They spoke for a couple of minutes—Mack giving the guy some kind of compliment, judging by the pleased grin on the other man's face—before Mack strolled back to me.

"Ready now?" I asked when he got back to the table.

"Yeah, sorry," he said. "I just wanted to tell him how much I liked the arrangement he did on that last song."

I couldn't help but smile at that. He'd probably made the guy's week.

Outside the pub, it was surprisingly chilly. A fresh, cold breeze had started blowing in off the sea. Mack paused on the pub steps to zip up his jacket.

"Where do you live, then?" he asked once we'd headed off.

"Not far from your B&B," I said. "My flat's pretty close to the sea front."

After we'd walked a bit further, he said, "It's a nice little town. Cute. Bloody quiet though."

"It can be," I agreed. "Especially in winter."

"Do you ever miss London?"

"Sometimes," I admitted. "Mostly when I want to do something like go clubbing, like last night. I've got to go all the way to Plymouth now for that and it's a bit of a drive, though I can at least stay with Gav, my mate."

"Yeah." Mack said. "Look, about last night . . ."

My heart started pounding with anticipation. "Yeah?"

He sighed. "You're not going to, you know, *say* anything?"

The wave of disappointment that swamped me was as surprising as it was ridiculous. What had I expected? To be invited up to his chintzy B&B bedroom for more amazing sex while his landlady listened outside the door? He was obviously only raising the subject to make sure there was no danger of me blabbing about what had happened between us to Mum and Derek.

I pasted a smile on face, though it felt awkward as hell. "Course not. It's just between us."

He nodded, gaze averted. Said softly, "Thanks."

And that was that.

As we walked on, in silence, I found myself musing on why he'd felt the need to check that point—was it possible Derek didn't know he was gay? That Mack was worried about breaking the news? Maybe I should tell him that Derek already knew about me and it wasn't something he had a problem with?

Eventually, I blurted out, "Does your dad not know? That you're gay, I mean?"

"Oh, he knows," Mack's tone was grim. That surprised me. I wanted to know more, but there was a finality, a *warning*, in his tone that was clearly intended to discourage further questions.

We had reached my turn-off by now and, reluctantly, I slowed my pace. I pointed up the side street. "This is me."

He stopped. "Oh, right."

"The sea front's only a couple of minutes down the hill. Take a left when you get there. It's about five minutes' walk to the White Rose."

Mack nodded. "Thanks. I'll say goodnight then."

"Yeah, night." Impulsively, I stuck out my hand and after a moment, he took it. His hand was warm, his grip firm. When our eyes met, I was struck again by how very appealing I found him, and felt an unexpected pang, as though at a loss.

Why did he have to be Derek's son?

Our hands separated and fell back to our sides.

"I'll see you tomorrow, then?" I hadn't intended it to be a question, but somehow an inquiring note crept in at the end.

"Yeah, I said I'd go up to your mum's place after breakfast. She was anxious for me to get back there early doors tomorrow."

"She's pretty stressed," I explained. "She won't sleep tonight, worrying."

Mack tilted his head, his expression curious. "Worrying about what? Me running off?"

I sighed. "Probably, yeah. Don't be offended—this whole thing's been really hard on her—she's not completely rational right now. Rosie's her baby."

He shrugged. "It's fine—I understand. And I won't be running off, okay? I may have issues with my dad, but that doesn't come into it. If I can help Rosie, I will."

Something about the way he said that, how his steady gaze met mine as he spoke, convinced me.

"Okay," I said.

He turned away then, lifting a hand in a final farewell as he began ambling down the hill, calling over his shoulder, "Goodnight."

"Night," I replied, though I didn't move. Just stood there and watched him till he turned the corner and was out of sight.

He didn't look back.

PROOF

CHAPTER EIGHT

Mack was a match.

Weirdly, the news surprised me. Maybe it was because there had been so many blows by then: first, the mystery of Rosie's illness, then the diagnosis, then the news that none of us could help her. But now, for the first time in what felt like forever, there was good news. Mack *could* help her.

He could save her life.

The process was quick. Mack had to undergo a raft of physical tests and scans but these were arranged swiftly and within days, we had a green light. The main delay arose after that, when the hospital insisted that Mack speak with a counsellor and take some time to reflect on his decision before confirming he wanted to proceed.

The night after he met with the counsellor, Mack announced his intention to visit a friend in Essex for a bit.

"The last thing you need is me sitting around here twiddling my thumbs while I weigh all this up," he'd said firmly.

He was wrong though. While he was gone, Rosie's mood was reached a new low and Mum got so stressed, I began to worry she might be heading for a breakdown. I'd never seen her in such a state. As for Derek, he was walking around like a zombie, unable to concentrate on anything.

For my part, I focused on the practicalities—someone had to hold everything together after all, and it wasn't like there was much else I could do, so I threw myself into running Dilly's, insisting that Mum and Derek prioritise Rosie. When I wasn't working double shifts at the café, I was at the Costco or paying bills or banking takings . . . I even washed the bloody windows one day. That's one good thing about running your own business. You never run out of things to do.

Six days later, Mack came back.

He arrived at the house on the Thursday evening and announced that he definitely wanted to go ahead.

After that, things moved fast.

The surgery date was quickly arranged—it was sobering to realise how pressing the doctors considered the procedure to be—along with a bunch of other pre-surgery appointments. Over the two weeks leading up to surgery, it felt like Rosie and Mack were constantly at the hospital having something tested or scanned or measured. Mum and Derek were at pretty much at every appointment which left me holding the fort at the café.

It was fine. Someone had to keep our employees in work and our customers coming through the doors, but yeah, there were times, occasionally, when I wished it didn't always have to be me; when I wished I wasn't constantly on the outside of what was happening with my sister. In my worst moments, I'd wonder if Rosie thought I didn't care and that I was more concerned about keeping Dilly's running. I knew she thought I was obsessed by the business—she was always rolling her eyes when I went round to hassle Mum and Derek about incomplete paperwork and unpaid bills. But right then, quite honestly, I couldn't have cared less about it. It was just that looking after the café was the only way I could contribute to our family crisis. It wasn't as if I could tag along to the appointments.

Not like Mack.

And God, what kind of a dick was I to feel resentful of that? Mack was giving her his fucking liver.

I wasn't *really* resentful. But sometimes, I'd go round in the evening, and I'd walk into the living room, and there they would be, the four of them, and they'd look up and I'd feel like . . .an interloper.

And sometimes, just *sometimes*, the idea would flash across my mind—*He's the interloper, not me.*

It would be a fleeting thought, banished an instant later. I knew it was dickish and stupid and untrue to boot. Unkind. But sometimes—well, yeah, that was how I felt.

A couple of nights before the surgery was due to take place, I went round to the house after closing up the café, like I'd been doing every night that week. When I walked in, the four of them were mid-conversation—or rather, Mum was mid-rant. She had a determined expression on her face and her voice had gone up in pitch, the way it did when she was agitated. Derek was sitting, silent and plainly uncomfortable, on the sofa beside her and Rosie was slouched miserably in her favourite armchair.

Mack, who appeared to be the victim of her rant, looked hunted.

"It's six weeks' recovery time," Mum was telling him. "It makes sense. You need someone to take care of you and you've admitted yourself you can't afford to stay at the B&B any longer."

"What's up?" I asked settling myself down in the only remaining vacant chair.

Mum glanced at me, "We're talking about where Dylan's going to stay after the surgery. It's obvious he should come here. We've got loads of room and I'll be running around after Rosie anyway. I may as well run after two as one."

"But I'm not going to bed-ridden," Mack protested. "I don't need a nurse."

"Then why not stay here?" I asked. "There's a spare room, and Mum would love to have you. You can't stay at the B&B for six weeks."

"That's what I said!" Mum exclaimed. She sent Mack a reproachful look. "I don't know why you won't let us help you?"

Mack stared at his hands while a dark red flush crept up his neck. He appeared as uncomfortable as Derek, ready to crawl under a rock.

Like father, like son.

Of course, being me, Mr. Fixer, I had to step in and try to make it better. Smooth over Mum's offended hurt; offer another explanation. Mediate.

I turned to her. "I can understand where Mack's coming from—he doesn't want to take up your time when you need to be concentrating on Rosie. She's going to need all your attention after surgery."

Mack glanced up, his expression grateful. "Yeah. That's it." He offered Mum his usual diffident shrug. "Rosie should be your priority when we get out. You can't be running after me as well."

"I don't mind," Mum said, but there was a note of doubt in her voice now.

"Besides," Mack went on firmly, "I'll be up and about pretty quickly and—"

For the first time since I'd arrived, Derek spoke up, interrupting Mack mid-sentence, his tone flat and uncompromising. "The doctor said you need to factor in a full six-week recovery period, son."

Mack's gaze snapped to his dad, his expression hardening, till eventually, Derek flushed and glanced away. The hostility coming off Mack was palpable.

"She also agreed that someone who's young and in decent shape might recover faster than that," Mack pointed out. "And frankly, Dad, I don't intend to hang around here for six whole weeks."

"I know you can't wait to leave," Derek said bleakly, "But you can't just go running off the day after your surgery, or even the next week—first, you need to give your body a chance to get over this. They're cutting out half your liver, for Christ's sake! It's a major operation. Not something to take lightly." His voice went hoarse on the last words. Then he added, more briskly, "Besides, like they told you, you won't be discharged till they do the three-month scan to check your liver's grown back properly."

Mack exhaled sharply. "Listen—" he began, and somehow I knew he wasn't going to give in. For whatever reason—and yes, I could guess why, we probably all could—he didn't want to stay under the same roof as Derek. But no way could we leave him to fend for himself after surgery. He was mad if he thought we'd let that happen.

"Why don't you stay with me?" I blurted.

The words were out of my mouth before I'd thought them through. Before I'd considered my own brief and secret history with Mack.

He turned his head and stared at me, seeming stunned—though really, was it such a surprising suggestion? I barrelled on, not giving him a chance to disagree.

"I won't be able to wait on you hand and foot, like Mum would," I said, keeping my tone casual and unconcerned, "In fact, I won't even be in most of the time, but I assume you're okay to entertain yourself, till you're feeling well enough to get out and about, yeah?"

I'll leave you in peace.
You're free to go when you want.

I saw a little of the tension leaching out of him as I gave those throwaway assurances, the tight set of his shoulders slowly easing, the firm set of his jaw unclenching. He remained silent though, watching me with that dark, wary gaze.

God, those eyes, dark as bitter chocolate. He must've got them from his mother because Derek's were a startling blue. He was like Derek in other ways though: in height and build, both of them with the same thick, shiny hair, though Derek's was almost entirely silver now.

Both of them clamming up whenever conversations got difficult.

"Please, Dylan. Say you'll stay with Nathan." That was Rosie, perched now on the edge of her chair, her worried gaze fixed on Mack.

He said, almost imploringly, "Rosie, I don't think—"

"*Please,*" she repeated, and her eyes filled with tears. "I'll worry if you're on your own."

Good old emotional blackmail.

Mack held out for about five seconds, expression torn. Then he sighed, long and hard. "Okay, you win." He turned to me then, and his smile was careful. "Thanks for the offer, Nathan. I reckon I'll be taking you up on it."

He didn't look thankful though—he looked wary. And he wasn't the only one.

Mack moved into the flat the next day, while I was working at the café. Mum gave him the spare key and he brought his stuff over. By the time I got home at six, he seemed to have settled in—not that there was much settling in a guy with one rucksack and a guitar case needed to do.

I found him in the living room, bent over his guitar and half humming, half singing under his breath as he worked through a song I recognised but couldn't put name to. His long, agile fingers coaxed the melody from the strings with the casual ease of long experience, and even mumble-singing as he was, I could tell his voice was a low baritone with a promise of richness.

He mustn't have heard me come in. I stood in the living room doorway for a couple of minutes listening to him play before he clocked me and abruptly stopped.

"Oh, hi!" He looked flustered, setting set the guitar down on the empty half of the sofa beside him and standing up. "Sorry, I didn't see you there."

"Sit down," I said, stepping further into the room. "You don't have to stop playing, I was enjoying it. What was that song?" I settled myself into my favourite chair, toeing off my beatup Nikes.

He sat slowly, almost reluctantly. "It's a Blur song. I was just messing about."

"Oh yeah," I said, recognition dawning. "I know the one you mean now—it sounded really nice like that. Acoustic, I mean."

He gave me an stiff half-smile. "Thanks." He didn't move to pick up the guitar again though.

"So, did you find your room?" I asked.

"Uh, yeah, I think so. Lorraine said to use the one next to the bathroom?"

"That's right." I attempted breezy good humour. "Got everything you need?"

"Yeah, course. I don't need much. Just a bed, really." He visibly cringed then, as though I might think this bland remark was a come on. "That is"—he rubbed at the back of his neck and cleared his throat—"Um, you know."

Yeah, I did. At least I knew that this weird awkwardness arose out of our mutual awareness that we'd slept together not so long ago. And now we were going to be living together in this compact space. Passing each other on the way to and from the shower in the morning. Sharing the sofa if we both wanted to watch TV in the evening.

My living room suddenly felt tiny.

I lurched to my feet, plastering what felt like a very fake smile across my face. "I'm going to make a cuppa," I announced. "Do you want one?"

He blinked at me, as though surprised by my surge of energy. "Um, sure, okay."

"Great," I said, too brightly. "Back in a mo.'"

I headed into the kitchen, closed the door behind me, rested my forehead against the hard wood and groaned.

Fuck my life.

PROOF

CHAPTER NINE

The surgery was scheduled for first thing on Tuesday morning when I was due to open up the café. Tuesdays were quiet and usually I opened up by myself, but that day I asked Katie to come in—and thank god I did. I was a mess all day, totally distracted and fit for nothing.

Mum and Derek were at the hospital while the surgery was happening. We exchanged texts through the day as I waited impatiently for news. When my phone finally rang just after three, I jumped, fumbling it with shaking fingers, my heart already pounding.

"Mum?"

"It's me," Derek said. "Everything's fine. The surgeon said it went well. Rosie's just been taken to Recovery."

The relief was intense. "What about Mack?"

"He's in Recovery too. He's okay."

I let out a hard sigh. "Can I come up now? I haven't been able to concentrate all day."

"She's going to be out of it for a while," Derek said. "Why don't you come for visiting hours tonight? Seven?"

I was silent for a moment. Derek's assumption that Rosie was my only concern annoyed me.

"Is it the same visiting hours for both wards?" I asked calmly.

"I think so. Are you going to look in on Dylan too?"

"Of course. Why wouldn't I?"

There was a brief silence.

"Well, good," he said at last. "Lorraine will appreciate that. She wants to be there for him but she can't quite bring herself to leave Rosie's side right now."

I paused, debating whether to say anything else. This probably wasn't easy for Derek. It might not be the best time to raise the topic of how things stood between him and Mack. Nevertheless, I found myself asking slowly, "Aren't you going to see him?"

"The last person he'll want to see is me," Derek replied, his tone flat and certain.

"I'm sure—"

"I'll see you here at seven, Nathan."

He hung up without waiting for a response.

That evening, I went to see Rosie first. She was still groggy and looked small and very wan in her hospital bed. Mum sat on a plastic chair at the head of the bed holding her hand—the one without the tube sticking in the back of it—and Derek sat on her other side, stroking her hair. They'd both clearly been through the mill today, faces drawn with lack of sleep and worry, but there was a peace to them now that hadn't been there before the operation.

"Hey Ro!" I called softly as I approached the bed, setting a cuddly gorilla on the cabinet beside the bed.

She smiled weakly. "Hey!"

"How you doing?"

"Oh, *great*!" She laughed at her own sarcasm.

Derek said in a wry tone, "She's all drugged up. Take a seat."

He gestured at the last remaining chair which was larger and more comfortable than the basic ones he and Mum were sitting on, though further from Rosie. The patient's chair. As I sat myself down, I met Mum's gaze.

"You okay?" I asked.

She nodded and smiled. "I am now. This morning was hell though."

For the next half hour we were all pretty quiet and subdued, content just to sit with each other, be with each other. At last though, I stood.

"I'm going to look in on Mack."

Mum smiled, seeming relieved. "Oh, would you love? I popped

down earlier when he was first coming round but I'm not sure he'll remember. I'll go and see him again in a little while but I want to sit with Rosie while she's awake."

"Course," I said. "It's not a problem." I glanced at Derek. He was staring at the floor.

"He's in Ward 14," Mum said. "Just say you're family if anyone asks. You are brothers after all."

"*Step*brothers," I blurted. "And it's not like I even met him till a month ago."

She didn't seem to find my comment odd. "Well the nurses aren't to know, are they?"

I sighed. "I suppose not."

I left the three of them in their quiet huddle and headed for Ward 14, following the faded yellow arrows painted on the worn, Hospital-blue floor.

Unlike Rosie's single-occupancy room, this was a four-bed ward. Three of the four beds were occupied. The two nearest the door, facing each other, were taken up by a sleeping elderly gent and a faded man in late middle-age who lay, helplessly listening to the monologue of a woman of around the same age. The bed beside him was empty and Mack was in the one opposite that, semi-reclined on a pile of pillows, his face turned to the window.

"Hi," I said as I drew near. "How are you feeling?"

His head jerked towards me— He was clearly taken aback. "Nathan? I wasn't expecting to see you." His voice was slightly slurred.

I laughed but I was frowning a little too. "Really?"

He didn't answer that, brows pleated with confusion, and his honest bemusement at my arrival bothered me somehow. Were his expectations of us all really so low? Then again, should that surprise me given Derek's behaviour?

"Do you mind?" I asked, hovering uncertainly. "I wanted to check on how you're doing but if you'd rather be alone . . ."

He looked at me blankly, then down at his own body, as though wondering how to answer and I realised that, despite seeming far more alert than Rosie, he was still pretty out of it, probably with some strong drugs in his system.

"Tell you what—I'll sit with you for a bit," I said gently. "But just tell me to go anytime you want. I won't be offended, okay?"

Something in his expression softened and it made me feel like I'd said the right thing—made me feel good out of all proportion.

"'kay," he breathed.

He had the same big patient chair Rosie had, next to his bed. I tugged it round to face him so he wouldn't have to move his head to look at me, and sat down.

"How are you feeling?" I asked.

"I actually feel really good." He added by way of explanation, "I've had a lot of drugs."

"Tomorrow might be a different story," I warned.

He smiled. "Yeah, I know."

I wondered if he'd had surgery before, or if he'd read up on the procedure. There was so much I didn't know about him.

"How's Rosie?" he asked.

"Good," I said, smiling. "All drugged up, just like you."

He gave a laugh, then winced, then laughed again at his own wince, which made me chuckle too, even as I said, "You okay? You need anything?"

"Nah." But he smiled and his eyes, all dark and melty, were gentle on mine. It felt like his inhibitions had relaxed for the first time since he'd come to Porthkennack, and okay, it was probably the drugs, but it still made me happy. Made me feel like I could look at him the way I wanted to look at him all the time.

"You've done a really good thing," I said.

He gave a little sigh. "I wish everyone would stop saying that. I just did what anyone would, getting a letter like that."

I watched him for a moment. "I don't think that's true, you know. You've not seen Derek for years—in all the time he's been married to my Mum, you and I have never met till now, and that's been, what? Sixteen years? You could easily have turned round and told Derek you wanted nothing to do with him or Rosie."

He glanced at me. His expression was thoughtful but I couldn't read it. Couldn't guess what he was thinking.

"Why would I do that?"

I paused. "Mum told me that the last time you saw Derek, you said you didn't want to see him anymore. That sounds like a reason."

For a long while, he didn't say anything—his expression didn't even alter. Then he sighed. "Is that what he told her?"

It was then I knew I'd made a mistake. This was not the time to be asking him about this stuff. I opened my mouth to change the subject but he spoke before I could get a word out.

"I suppose I did say that." His voice was oddly dreamy. "But that last time . . . it was at my mum's funeral. He sat at the back. Then, after the service, he came up and asked me if I was okay. We'd had this big argument the night before and I just . . . well, I just lost it. Screamed at him to fuck off." He gave short laugh, then winced again.

I knew I should stop him but I wanted to hear this, wanted to know the worst, so I stayed quiet and let him go on.

"I'd never got angry like that at my dad before, but once I started, I couldn't stop. It all came out. I told him I hated him, said I never wanted to see him again." He paused. "I remember I told him that he hadn't acted like a dad to me for years so what was the point pretending he cared because Mum had died?"

Abruptly he fell silent. My throat felt thick with emotion and I didn't know what to say. I couldn't imagine what that must have been like for him. To be fifteen and feel so alone.

Mack said, "He didn't even argue with me, you know? Just . . . stared at me. Then he turned round and walked out the church. And that was the last time I saw him." He sighed. "Till now."

"Jesus, Mack," I muttered. "I'm so sorry. I had no idea."

I couldn't comprehend it, couldn't take it in. That Derek had been so easily turned away by his own son, a boy whose words had obviously been prompted by grief and hurt—it shocked me.

Derek had been a good stepdad to me, and he was pretty great dad to Rosie. But to Mack?

Fuck.

Was it fair to judge Derek? Maybe not, but I couldn't help doing just that.

I thought back to that long-ago conversation with Mum and wondered how much she knew about what had really happened between Derek and Mack. Had Derek shared all the details with her? Surely she'd known he'd gone up there for his ex's funeral?

Had she?

One thing about my mum—she adored Derek. At the height of the Dilly's crisis, we'd had a few arguments over how unreliable he was, and she'd always defended him and expected me to excuse his behaviour. She used to say privately to me that he was like a little boy beneath the confident exterior, easily hurt, deceptively soft. She'd mentioned that his own childhood had been somehow, mysteriously, "difficult". And maybe it had. What did I know? Could someone like me, secure and happy and doted on my two parents, ever really understand?

But when I saw Mack, half-reclining against the mound of pillows in his hospital bed, eyes close, I felt so angry on his behalf. Not to mention guilty. Guilty that, while Derek had been playing happy families with Mum and me and Rosie, Mack had been left behind. Forgotten.

Mack's lashes quivered and he opened his eyes again. He looked right at me, oddly unguarded in this moment. It seemed that exhaustion was setting in now—there were shadows under his eyes, weariness in every line of his body.

"Do you want me to go?" I asked.

For several beats, he said nothing, then he murmured through barely moving lips. "You can a stay a little longer." Pause. "If you like."

"Hold me."

"All right," I said. "I'll stay till you fall asleep."

For a while we sat quietly, then he said, "I was okay after the funeral, you know."

"Were you?"

"Course. I went to live with my gran and grandad."

"In Perth?"

"Nah, they lived in Glasgow." So that had been another move for him.

Mack's eyes tracked my face unselfconsciously. Right now, there was no awkwardness between us. The wariness I'd grown used to seeing on his face was gone and his mouth had an uncharacteristically relaxed set that made his lips soft and kissable.

And, Christ, why was I letting my mind go *there*?

I cleared my throat. "Did you get on with your grandparents?"

"They were okay," he said, his tone non-committal. "They made sure I had everything I needed. They were just set in their ways. They didn't approve of me being gay. Anyway, it wasn't for that long. I left when I was seventeen."

Not exactly a glowing reference. The renewed burst of rage I felt towards Derek startled me. Because really, why should it bother me so much that Mack had been neglected by his dad? Mack himself seemed pretty philosophical about it, even with his inhibitions down.

Was he though?

"I'm not here for a reunion, Dad."

Since the day he'd arrived in Porthkennack, Mack had avoided spending any time with Derek, to the extent that even when Derek was around, he would address most of his remarks to Mum.

No, he probably wasn't philosophical about the situation with Derek. Not deep down.

I couldn't help wondering how he felt about me. While he'd been left to his own devices, I'd had the benefit of both my own parents and Derek in my life. Mack had had no one by the sounds of it.

Mack closed his eyes again. He was pale with exhaustion. I was surprised he'd stayed awake as long he had, looking as tired as he did, and with all the drugs in his system. Even like this though, looking far from his best, I still found him unbelievably appealing. There was something about Mack MacKenzie that just got to me. It wasn't only his appearance—though yeah, I liked the way he looked a *lot*—it was something about the man underneath. He had to have strength of character to have come here, to Porthkennack, to help the sister he'd never met, despite his history with his dad. I admired that a lot. And then there were those hints of fragility he occasionally showed. That he was showing right now. Those got to me in a different way.

Damn, I really was a fixer.

More than anything, I wanted to drive away the shadows that I saw in his eyes. Wanted to mend the rift between him and Derek. Wanted to see if I could coax him to smile, genuinely smile. Laugh too, raucously, holding nothing back. I wondered if he ever did that. It occurred to me that I'd give a lot to see that.

I watched him for a few minutes, waiting to see if he'd open his eyes again. He didn't. He just lay there, almost unnaturally still. I was pretty sure he'd fallen asleep, but I'd said I'd stay till he did, so I wanted to be sure.

"Do you want me to leave?" I whispered softly.

He didn't answer. His face was peaceful. I could practically see the lines of tiredness ironing out.

I sat there for another few minutes, waiting for a nurse to come along. Finally one did, cheerful and bustling in green scrubs.

"Is he sleeping?" she asked, making no effort to lower her voice. I glanced at Mack anxiously but he didn't move a muscle.

"Looks like it," I said, getting to my feet. "I should leave."

She smiled at me. "You must be the brother." She winked conspiratorially. "I was speaking to your mum earlier. She said you might pop by."

I stared at her. I wanted to say, *I'm not his brother*, but the words wouldn't come. Instead I gave her a strained smile. "I'll pop by again tomorrow."

"He should be less tired then," she assured me, twitching the curtains round the bed.

The metal rings clattered as she tugged them round the rail but it didn't matter.

Mack didn't so much as stir.

CHAPTER
TEN

PROOF

Months have passed since you were last
The lover I once lost myself in
I can't believe it's Christmas Eve
And soon a new year will begin
All I can think as I sit here drinking
Is whether you'll be here by Spring
Or if you'll go and leave me low
If you do that, babe, I won't have anything
(Repeat chorus)
Christmas Stocking by The Sandy Coves, 1989

September

The next few days passed quickly. The café was busy without Mum and Derek to help out. They spent all their time at the hospital, mostly with Rosie, though Mum forced Derek to go with her to see Mack each afternoon. I got in the habit of visiting Rosie after the lunchtime rush when they were with Mack, then I'd drop in on Mack in the evening, once the café had closed.

It was obvious early on that he was set on being released as soon as possible. He pushed himself hard, first to get up out of bed, then to start walking around, ignoring the nurses' warnings that he needed to pace himself. Although he never complained of any pain to me, I'd see him steeling himself before he stood up or took a step, his grim expression telling. In those first few days after the surgery, the simplest of activities exhausted him, a fact that clearly frustrated the hell out of him.

"You're going to have to resign yourself to letting me do *some* things for you for a couple of weeks," I told him one evening, a few days after the operation. I helped myself to a few Malteasers from the family bag sitting on his bedside cabinet, tossing one up and catching it in my mouth.

"Ugh, unhygienic!"

"Unhygienic how?" I demanded, tossing another chocolate ball in the air. I caught that one too then displayed it to him between my teeth, grinning.

"This is a hospital—it's full of bloody germs!"

"What, my Malteasers are going to pick up germs as they travel through the air?" I chuckled.

He just rolled his eyes and it made me smile. He'd eased up in my company these last few days, and I liked it. I liked it a lot.

"Anyway," I went on, "the point is, you're going to need to some help when you first get out of here." I waggled my eyebrows at him. "So, if you want me to give you a bedbath, you let me know. Because I can absolutely do that."

He gave me the repressive look he used on me whenever I said something joke-flirty like that. "I just need to take things slowly for a bit," he said. "I'll be fine."

"It's not a crime to ask for help, you know," I said, tossing another Malteaser up and catching it. "You just need to ask."

They finally agreed to release him on the sixth day. He'd been haranguing the nurses about getting released—I was convinced they only agreed in the end because they couldn't take any more of his increasingly irascible questions.

I arranged to extend Katie's shift so I could go to pick him up and take him back to the flat. When I arrived at the ward, he was sitting in the chair beside his bed, fully dressed with his packed rucksack beside him.

When he saw me approaching the bed, he got slowly, determinedly, to his feet.

"Thank God you're here," he said. "I can't wait to get out of here. I need a burger."

I laughed. "I suppose we could stop off at Macky Ds if you're desperate."

"Cool your heels, Speedy," said a voice behind me. I turned. It was the nurse from the first night. She was in her usual scrubs plus a green plastic apron. She stepped past me, offering an unappetising tray of hospital food to Mack. "You'll have to wait for the doctor to sign your release forms and her round's not till two. Here's your lunch."

"She said I could go home last night!" Mack protested.

The nurse shrugged, clearly unmoved. "She's still got to sign the forms, hon.'"

Mack muttered out a string of curses that I couldn't make out but was willing to bet were fantastically rude. The nurse just laughed.

"Fine." Mack scowled. "But I'm going to see my sister till the round starts. If I sit here a moment longer, I'll go mad."

"I'll get you a wheelchair," the nurse said, but Mack waved her off, getting to his feet and making for the door.

"I'll walk."

"You should have taken the wheelchair," I told him a few minutes later when he stopped in the middle of the corridor, expression drawn, gingerly touching his side. "You've been told to take it easy—they're not giving you that advice for the good of their own health, you know."

Mack glared at the pale green vinyl floor, saying nothing.

I sighed. "We're nearly there. Lean on me for now. I'll find a wheelchair for the return journey while you and Rosie chat."

With a grudging look, Mack let me slide my arm round his waist while he propped his over my shoulder. He was slim but solid, a surprisingly heavy weight. I liked the way he leaned on me though, and, when I turned my head, the faint scent of tea tree from his shampoo. He'd been complaining about not being allowed to shower the night before. The nurses must've relented this morning.

Right then, an image popped into my mind, of Mack standing naked under a shower spray. My cock began to twitch and fill, which was fucking awkward given that he was pressed up against me.

I suppressed a curse. Jesus, what was wrong with me? Clearly, it had been way too long since I'd had sex. And of course, that thought made me recall exactly when the last time had been: with Mack, at his hotel. The memory didn't help my erection subside.

Determinedly, I shoved my predicament out of my mind and began slowly walking, supporting Mack as we went.

"Have you seen Rosie since the op?" I asked in a desperate attempt to distract myself.

"Once," he said. "Well, twice, but the first time she was sleeping. Dad brought me down in a wheelchair." He paused. "She looked pretty awful both times."

"Her recovery's going to take longer than yours," I pointed out. "She's been poorly for months now, but the doctors seem pleased with her progress."

He glanced at me, hopefully. "You think?"

I found I wanted, *needed*, to reassure him. "She'll be fine, Mack. You've made sure of that."

He swallowed, hard. "There's always a chance of rejection though. It's weird but I feel . . .it's like I feel responsible for her getting better, you know? Like, it's my liver in her, and if it doesn't make her better, it's my fault?" We'd reached the door of Rosie's ward now—she'd been moved out of her single room after the first couple of days. I stopped walking and turned so that I faced Mack while still carefully supporting him with my arm.

"Listen," I said. "Things weren't looking too good till you came along. Rosie didn't have a donor. She was basically waiting for someone to die. Even if this doesn't work out, you've at least given her a fighting chance. None of us were able to do that."

Mack met my gaze. He didn't say anything but his dark eyes were understanding, like he knew how hard that had been for me.

"Okay," he said at last. "Let's go and see her."

Rosie was curled up in the big chair next to her bed playing on her phone when we got to her ward. Derek was reading the paper. He looked up when we arrived, then hurriedly got to his feet, gesturing at the ridiculously uncomfortable visitor chair he'd been using.

"Dylan, sit down here."

"I don't need—"

"Sit," I said firmly, giving him a little shove.

He scowled at me, but did as I said.

Rosie snorted with amusement. "Nathan's so like Mum," she told Mack. "The two of them are unbelievably bossy, aren't they, Dad?"

Derek smiled weakly at Rosie. "Yeah. For sure."

His discomfort was palpable, the tension between him and Mack thick enough you could cut it with a knife. From what I'd seen, Mack didn't seem to know how to treat Derek at all, always stiff and awkward around him. As for Derek, he gave off the vibe that he'd rather be somewhere—anywhere—else. Which probably didn't help with dispelling Mack's obvious conviction that Derek didn't given a shit about him.

Was it possible Mack was right? Did Derek's behaviour genuinely reflect his feelings? Surely not—whatever his faults, I didn't believe Derek didn't care about Mack.

Mack and Rosie were on the same level now, both sitting. Mack asked Rosie what she was doing on her phone and she started showing him, swiping at the screen with her quick fingers. He was good like that, with her. Didn't talk at her the way adults so often did with kids, asking them question after question like it was an interview, controlling the conversation—like I did, really. He just let her show him her stuff and natter about it, asking the odd question during the lulls.

I had a feeling I was about to lose my favourite brother spot.

I wasn't sure how I felt about that. Or how Mack did. He'd surprised me, with how much he seemed to want to get know Rosie, especially when he didn't seem to feel that way about the rest of us. I admitted, I wished he wanted to get to know me better. Whilst he'd grown more friendly over the last few days, there was still a distance there, a line he stayed firmly behind.

I watched them, two dark heads bent together over the little screen. Then I turned to Derek.

"How's Mum today?"

"Better," he said. "I packed her off to the hairdressers his afternoon. You know how she is though—she was refusing to go till Rosie told her point blank she needed to get her bloody roots sorted out." He laughed warmly and I saw Mack glance up. He had a great laugh, did Derek. Infectious. Something about it just made you smile and wonder what was funny.

After a bit, I slipped off in search of a wheelchair for Mack. It took me a while to track one down but eventually I was back at Rosie's bedside with my prize.

"Your carriage awaits," I told Mack, gesturing at the wheelchair.

Mack grimaced. "I can walk."

"Nope," I said firmly. "We agreed on the way down here that we'd be taking wheels back to Ward 14—and by the way, we'll also be taking them out to the car." When he opened his mouth to protest I ploughed on. "That's non-negotiable, my friend."

Rosie laughed again and my heart warmed to see her eyes glinting with real humour. It felt like months since I'd seen her like this, and so soon after surgery, it felt like a miracle.

Mack wasn't laughing though—he was grimacing as he levered himself up and again as he dropped into the wheelchair. "Fine, I'll use the bloody thing," he gritted out, "But only to get out of this place, then I'm back to my own two feet."

"At least you're getting out," Rosie said. "I'll be stuck here a couple more days at least." She scowled. "I can't wait to go home. The food's awful and they wake you up at the crack of dawn for breakfast and make you go to sleep super-early at night. It's like being a little kid."

Her expression was disgusted but there was no real fire in her.

I went to her and hugged her. I wanted to hug her tight but she was too sore for that, so I contented myself with a gentler embrace and pressing a kiss to the top of her head.

When I broke away, turning back to the wheelchair where Mack sat waiting, I caught an oddly poignant look on his face that brought a lump to my throat.

Hold me.

On the other side of the bed, Derek sat, staring down at his loosely linked hands.

CHAPTER ELEVEN

By the time we got back to the flat, Mack was grey with exhaustion. He'd KB'd the hospital lunch tray and we'd skipped the Macky Ds plan so I suggested we have some lunch.

"To be honest, I could do with a nap first," he said.

"Okay. Do you need any help?" I hesitated. "You know, with your clothes or anything?"

He didn't seem to register my embarrassment. Too tired probably. "Nah, I'm fine," he said and headed for the bedroom like a zombie.

After a couple of hours, I tentatively looked in on him. He was sleeping on top of the covers in his clothes. I fetched a blanket and draped it over him, closing the door quietly after me.

It was a few more hours before he finally got up, bleary-eyed. I'd made chicken soup by then and he ate two bowls. He attempted to watch TV with me for a bit but after a series of jaw-cracking yawns, let me steer him back to bed. A minute after he lay down, he was out like a light.

He emerged from his bedroom at eleven the next morning, looking marginally better, though still pale. When I presented him with a breakfast of soft boiled eggs, he stared at the plate in disbelief.

"Soldiers? You made me toast soldiers?"

I blushed and glared at him. "What's wrong with that? I always have soldiers with boiled eggs. Doesn't everyone?"

He laughed. "No one over the age of ten, I reckon."

I didn't mind him teasing me though. It felt like a toe over that invisible line of his.

I was back to work today, though only for the lunch shift. Katie and Denise had agreed to put in a few extra hours to help out and I'd arranged the rota so I'd be home every day by four to check up on Mack.

The next few weeks passed uneventfully. Each day, Mack stayed awake a little longer and did a little more. He watched TV, played on the X-Box, noodled around on his guitar. I even caught him reading one of my books once, despite him having said he wasn't much of a reader.

It was a strangely relaxing time, not just for Mack but for me too. I'd cook dinner in the evenings and then we'd watch a movie or play X-Box, sitting side by side on the sofa, controllers in hand. Or we talked.

We talked a lot actually. Although Mack wasn't the chattiest guy in the world, he was an amazingly good listener, attentive and interested, always asking questions. He made me feel like whatever I was saying was fascinating. And although he was reluctant to talk about himself, I managed to wheedle some information out of him about his childhood.

He talked a bit about what happened after Derek first left his mum. They'd lived in Essex then and he'd still been seeing Derek, though it sounded like the visits had gradually decreased over the years, especially after Derek had moved to Cornwall. Then, when Mack had been thirteen, his mum got a job as a live-in warden in a sheltered housing complex in Perthshire, in her native Scotland. He wasn't really up for talking about how he'd felt about that move, but from his reticence, I suspected it hadn't been a great time for him. It wasn't the best age to move schools after all.

"Turning up for my first day at a Scottish secondary school with an Essex accent wasn't much fun," was as close he got to admitting it though.

He downplayed most things actually. I worked out that his mum had probably fallen ill a year or so after they got to Scotland. They had moved in with his grandparents in Glasgow a few months before she died.

He'd been fifteen then, to my sixteen. At the other end of the country, I'd been studying for my GCSEs, going to swimming and football training every week, playing a league game every Sunday. Prompted by the adults around me, I'd been thinking about what A levels I should do, what university I wanted to eventually go to, what I wanted to do with my life.

Things had plainly been very different for Mack.

"I left when I was seventeen . . ."

Where had he gone? I wanted to know that next part of his story, but he didn't offer and it felt wrong to ask. That was something he held quite far back behind his line.

By the Friday of the third week, Mack was itching to go out. I got back from work that day to find him putting on his trainers.

"Where are you going?"

"I need some air," he told me in a fractious tone. "I'm fed up looking at the same four walls."

I'd brought snacks on the way home for the *Aliens* movie night we'd planned. I took them through to the kitchen and dumped them on the table, then headed back into the living room. He was standing now, rubbing the back of his neck with one hand in that gesture that meant he felt uncomfortable. My stomach flipped at the sight of him, all long and lean in his soft, worn jeans and beat-up jacket.

"I'll come with you," I said.

"You don't want to do that, You've just got back from work and you've been on your feet all day. I'll be fine."

He was clearly determined not to inconvenience me, and okay, I didn't *really* want to go out for a walk right now, but I did want to go with him. He was tons better than he'd been even just a week before, but he was still wincing from time to time when he moved around.

"Come on, it'll be nice," I said in a cheerful tone. "We'll stroll down to the sea front and get an ice cream or a coffee or something."

He smiled, and for an instant, I was sure I saw a flash of . . .relief? Or maybe gratitude? I don't know, but it made me glad I'd insisted on going with him.

"Okay, coffee," he said gruffly. "It's too cold for ice cream today."

"Hey, it's never too cold for ice cream!" I scolded teasingly.

It took about three times longer than usual to walk down to the sea front. Mack started off at his usual pace but soon had to slow down.

"God, this is ridiculous," he complained. "I should be better by now."

"It's only been three weeks," I pointed out. "You need to be patient. You're a lot better already but they did say you needed six weeks recovery time minimum."

Mack sighed and shoved his hands deeper in his pockets. I wished I could . . . I don't know, I suppose I wished I could put my arm round him. Instead I contented myself with a shoulder bump, prompting another of those rare smiles.

Shit, I had it bad for Mack MacKenzie. Which was, well, not the best, considering he clearly had no interest in me.

When we got to the sea front, I sat Mack down on an empty bench then jogged over to the Square Peg Café to fetch us a couple of coffees, ignoring the waitress's boot-faced scowl when I asked her to put the drinks in takeaway cups. I ordered a skinny latte for me and a filter with a dash for Mack—he didn't like 'milky coffee'—then, on impulse, added a chocolate brownie to go. Mack could do with a bit of fattening up.

By the time I got back to the bench, Mack looked like he was freezing in his thin bomber jacket. I knew he'd refuse my warmer one if I offered it, so instead, I satisfied myself with handing him the hot coffee, which would at least warm his hands, and gradually fed him the brownie. I knew by now that if I tried to simply hand him the brownie, he'd say he didn't want it. But I'd discovered that if I offered him treats like that less conspicuously, bit by bit while chatting, he'd happily eat them up.

We sat there on our bench, gazing out to sea, swilling down our third-rate coffee as the sun crept towards the horizon.

"You know." Mack said after a while. "I don't think I've said thanks to you, for putting me up. You've been really generous about it and it's not like you knew me before all this."

I glanced at him, uncomfortable. "No need to thank me," I replied. "You saved Rosie's life, for God's sake. And you're family." I felt odd as soon as those last words left my mouth, not because they weren't true—they were. Mack *was* family—but they brought up the idea of our being step-brothers and that absolutely wasn't how I thought of him.

He didn't respond to that, just stared out to sea. I watched him surreptitiously. He had a very nice profile, did Mack.

"Do you think you could put up with me another week?" he asked at last, his tone diffident.

"Only a week?" I said, frowning. "I assumed you'd be staying with me till you were recovered."

He turned to me then and I saw his throat bob. "I should head off. I need to get back to earning. I'm almost out of cash."

I blinked at him. "You can't . . . you can't seriously be thinking about *working*, Mack?"

He immediately looked away, eyes on the horizon again. "Why not?"

"It's only been three weeks since the op!" I exclaimed. "You're not fit!"

"It'll be a month by next week," he said stubbornly.

I huffed out a breath. "The doctors said you needed six weeks to recover. *At least* six weeks and not going back to work for eight to twelve weeks. You need to wait for the all-clear scan too. You know all this, Mack. You shouldn't be thinking of working yet."

"Yeah, well, I'm skint, okay?" he shot back, cheeks flushing. "So I need to get on my feet a bit quicker."

"No, you don't. You're staying with me, so you've got no bills to worry about."

He shook his head in swift negation. "I can't leech off you—"

"It's not leeching!" I protested. "Mack, you can't think that!" It genuinely upset me that he thought that way, and the surprise on his face told me he saw how horrified I was.

He stared at me helplessly. "I feel like I'm taking advantage, living here, eating your food, using your stuff."

"Mack, you're family," I said again, laying my hand on his knee. Even as I did so, I was aware of a frisson of excitement, just from that simple touch, and I cursed inwardly because, yeah, my attraction to him complicated this. At my end, anyway. At his end—who knew? I couldn't tell.

He sighed, as though in acknowledgement of all I'd said, but he still looked unhappy. And I knew why. He clearly found it hard to accept things from others. It had been nothing to him to give away half his liver to Rosie, but he'd rather flog himself to death, working for minimum wage, than live rent-free at my place.

I said, searching for some kind of fix, "Listen, how about if you help me out?"

"Doing what?"

He had me there. I wracked my brains, thinking of all the stuff I did for Dilly's week-in, week-out. Trying to think of something Mack could do from the flat without tiring himself too much.

"I could help out in the café, I suppose," he offered, tentatively. "I've done tons of waiting and kitchen work. And I was a barista for a few months—you do coffee, don't you?"

I frowned. "That's work, Mack! You'd be on your feet all day. It'd be way too much for you right now."

He looked weirdly gutted. Maybe he felt excluded from the whole Dilly's thing? After all, me, Mum and Derek all worked there, and Rosie had talked about doing some shifts in the summer holidays in one of her brighter moments recently.

"Could you—" I began, and then inspiration struck. "Could you come and play sometimes?"

"Play," he said flatly. Then, "What, my guitar?"

"Yeah," I said. "Why not? Some low-key music would be nice. If you're up to it, that is. We'd need to get you sitting down though. Like when you play at home."

He scowled. "I can play fine, but don't you think it would be weird? In an ice cream parlour?"

I shook my head. "Not at all, I was thinking late weekday afternoons—that's our quietest time off-season. It might bring in a few more customers in at the end of the day. A bit of entertainment. What do you say?"

He stared at me, unyielding. "I think it's weird."

I laughed. "Well, maybe it is—but is that a reason not to do it? I'm prepared to give something weird a go to see if we can get a little business in the door. I'd rather do that than close earlier Monday to Wednesday, which is the other option I was considering now that tourist season is winding up. Earlier closing means cutting the part-timers' hours and I don't like doing that if I can help it." That much was true.

Mack studied me, his expression serious. At last he shrugged. "Okay, fine. If that's what you want."

"Great," I said, grinning at him. "It is."

PROOF

CHAPTER TWELVE

Mid September

Mack gave his first café performance a week later. We picked Wednesday afternoon, from four till five since that coincided with one of my shifts. After I suggested the slot, I worried I might be asking too much—what if he didn't have enough polished material for a whole hour? Was I making unfair assumptions just because he carried a guitar around with him? He hadn't seemed perturbed by performing when I'd suggested it though, so I had to assume it would be okay.

I asked Katie, who usually finished up at three, to stay on a bit that day so I could pop back to the flat and carry Mack's gear for him—I still wouldn't let him lift anything heavier than a mug of tea, much to his frustration. He was tucking his arms through the straps of his guitar case when I got there. We tussled over it for a few seconds till he eventually gave up with a sigh and let me have my way.

"Do you have any music you need to take?" I asked as we headed for the door of the flat, hoping that might give me a clue as to what he planned.

"Nah."

That was it. *Nah.*

The thing was, I was nervous for him. I knew he could play. I'd heard him play a lot in the flat by now, but he just tended to noodle around, doing a bit of this or that tune, or working away at a tricky part for ages. He'd never actually straight out *performed* anything for me. What if he wasn't—well, any good? I hated the idea of people talking about him under their breath—*Oh my god, who* is *this guy?* I didn't even know why I felt so protective of him. It was ridiculous.

When we were halfway there, I couldn't hold back my curiosity any longer.

"So," I said breezily, "Have you decided what you're going to play?"

He sent me an amused glance. "What do you think?"

"I don't know," I said breezily. "I've heard you playing all sorts at home—folk, pop, rock."

"Are you worried?" His grin was teasing now.

"No, of course not. I trust you."

He laughed.

"What?"

"You know you're a control freak, don't you?" he said, but he was smiling at me almost fondly. "Look, why don't you tell me what you'd like me to play?"

I frowned. "Isn't a bit late for that? We're on our way there now."

"I'm pretty versatile."

A double entendre sprang to mind at that but I managed to leave it unsaid. Instead I said, "Okay, how about Justin Bieber? I'm sure that would go down well."

He laughed at that. "Touché!"

Weirdly though, that conversation did settle me down. Mack was obviously confident about what he was about to do and didn't feel out of his depth.

When we got to the café, only about half the tables were occupied, all by regulars. I asked Katie to deal with the customers while I did some paperwork and left Mack to set himself up in the corner. He prompted a few curious glances from the table of young mums who came in around this time every day, but seemed unperturbed by the attention. I sat myself down at the small table nearest the counter with my laptop and a large cappuccino and surreptitiously watched him.

I didn't know what it was about Mack, but I enjoyed just watching him *do* stuff. Something about the economical, unhurried way he moved and his calm, unflappable demeanour. From the first he'd struck me as a laidback guy—the opposite of me, really, and maybe that was part of the attraction. Maybe I was drawn to him because his quietness soothed me. Sitting there, in the corner of Dilly's, fine-tuning his instrument, he seemed so relaxed, I couldn't help but smile. I'd been worried he'd be nervous, but no. Quite the opposite. In fact, I'd never actually seen him look more at home than he did right now. There was a sureness to him when he held his guitar that he didn't have when his hands were empty.

Katie leaned over the counter. She was only a couple of years older than Rosie but with her willowy height and heavy make-up, she could easily have passed for mid-twenties.

"What's he going to play?" she whispered.

I shrugged. "I have no idea."

Right then, Mack glanced up. He caught my eye, winked at me and started to play *Love Yourself*, by Justin Bieber.

And I laughed like an idiot.

It was quite a little gig in the end. After *Love Yourself*, Mack played a whole host of crowd pleasers: the Beatles, Ed Sheerhan, Johnny Cash. We got a few new customers who'd been attracted by the music, and stayed open till five-thirty. We didn't make a whole lot of money, but it was nice to bring people in with something other than the lure of ice cream and to have them sit a bit longer too.

And it was really nice to hear Mack play, his voice low and clean, his hands moving with practiced ease. The small crowd loved him, a few of them talking to him after he finished, and several asking me when he'd be on again.

He was smiling as we walked home.

"You're very talented," I told him. "Do you have, you know, plans in that direction?"

He shook his head. "Nah. I'm not ambitious."

"Have you ever been in a band?"

"A few. Every one of them ended badly. I think I'm more of a . . . solo artist, if you know what I mean?" He smiled at me. "A lone wolf."

"All wolves are pack animals at heart," I said. "Maybe you just never found the right . . . bandmates?"

His smile tightened. "Are we still talking about bands?"

I flushed. There was my fixer nature coming out again. "Sorry."

He shrugged. "It's okay." Then, after a beat, "But you should know—I really am a lone wolf, Nathan."

Mack played at the café again on the Monday and Wednesday of the next week. On Monday, we got a few extra customers, mostly people who'd been in the previous week and had wanted to come again. By the Wednesday though, word had got round and we were practically full.

Mum brought Rosie with her to listen on the Wednesday. They squeezed themselves in at my tiny table near the counter, forcing me to put away my laptop.

"Why didn't you tell us he was doing this?" Mum said as Mack tuned up in his usual, patient, all-the-time-in-the-world way.

I said, honestly, "He didn't want me to."

"Why not?"

I gave her a look.

"What?"

"You kind of make a fuss about things and, in case you've not noticed, he's not really into being fussed over."

She gasped. "I do not!"

I glanced at Rosie for support, but she clearly wasn't listening. Her gaze was fixed on Mack and there was a distinct gleam of hero-worship in her eyes that, I have to admit, I envied. Well, I was used to being the only big-brother-show in town.

I turned back to Mum. "So, where's Derek?"

"Oh, working," she said vaguely, and I definitely didn't imagine the flush of scarlet that stained her cheeks. Terrible liar, my mother.

"Does *he* know Mack's playing here?"

She eyed me, then glanced at Rosie, who still wasn't paying us the slightest bit of attention, before adding under her breath. "He thinks Dylan won't want him here. I told him not to be so silly, but, well . . ." She trailed off, as though unsure how to complete the thought, and no wonder because yes, there was some basis for Derek's fears.

Mack *did* go out of his way to avoid Derek, though I suspected his actions stemmed from his deep-rooted conviction that Derek didn't care about him. And really who could blame him? With how Derek was behaving, it didn't look as though that was a view Mack was likely to change anytime soon. Whatever Derek's reasons for staying away, Mack would probably interpret them as lack of interest.

My depressing thoughts were interrupted when Mack began to play. He started with an Ed Sheerhan song, which most of the crowd clearly knew well, immediately drawing them in. I glanced at Mum, unaccountably pleased by her obvious surprise at Mack's skill. As for Rosie, she was gazing at Mack worshipfully. She was a complete music fiend and had taken up guitar the year before she fell ill, though her lessons had fallen by the wayside a few months ago.

When Mack finished that first song, Rosie turned to me and said breathlessly, "He's way better than Dad. I think he might be better than my teacher!"

Mum gave a startled laugh. "Don't tell Dad that!"

Rosie giggled, but I didn't think Mum was kidding. Derek was pretty precious about his musician status. I had to wonder what he'd make of Mack's playing. Mack was good, no doubt. Versatile too. I'd heard Derek play quite a bit, but only rock and pop stuff. Mack could play anything: rock, country, folk, even classical. There was a natural ease to his playing, even in how he held the instrument, as though the guitar was an extension of his own body. As though he didn't need to think about the notes at all.

When Mack finished his set, Katie started closing down at the counter while Mum and I began clearing tables and gently encouraging the customers out the door. Rosie joined Mack as he packed his stuff up, chattering away to him as he worked. Mack didn't seem to be saying much, but he smiled at her, and put in the odd comment. She seemed to bloom under his quiet attention, talkative in a way she hadn't been for a long time. It warmed me to see her acting her old self again, but it was kind of painful too, to see how easily Mack could draw her out of herself when for the last few months, I'd barely been able to get a word out of her.

Finally, when the last customer had gone, and Katie had left, Mum and I joined Rosie and Mack.

"Dylan love, that was so good," Mum said, laying her hand on his arm. She laughed. "I suppose that's not so surprising—like father, like son."

Mack smiled stiffly at her. "Actually, my mum was a musician too. She was the one who taught me guitar."

Mum looked mortified. "Oh, right. I didn't think of that. Of course, that was how she and Derek met, wasn't it?"

"Yeah," Mack said shortly. "He had an affair with her while he was married to his first wife. Unfortunately, he got her up the duff, and that was the end of her music career."

Mum's face went scarlet.

"Mack, come on," I said wearily.

He sighed. "Sorry," he said flatly, not looking at any of us.

"No, no," Mum said, patting his arm again. "I understand." Though what she thought she understood, I wasn't sure.

Rosie, bless her, changed the subject back to Mack's playing. "That was so good, Dylan!" she gushed. "Will you teach me? I was getting lessons from this guy for a while—he's got his own band—but I stopped after I got properly ill and it's been ages since I practiced. I really want to start up again though! I want to play like you."

His expression was wary. "Um—I'm not sure that's such a great idea." He looked at me, as though for support, though why he imagined I'd back him up on this, I don't know. As for Mum, she was beaming again.

"I think it's a wonderful idea!" she said.

"Come on!" Rosie urged. "It'll give us a chance to *bond*." She giggled.

So spoke the adored younger child, secure of her place in the world. If Mack thought he was getting out this, he was deluded.

"The thing is," Mack said desperately. "I'm not going to be around for much longer."

Rosie smiled big. "Well there you go! That's all the more reason for us to spend time together while we can." She added, with youthful callousness, "I can go back to my old teacher once you've gone."

Mack cleared his throat. "Oh, right." He paused as though waiting for some last reprieve. When none came, he sighed. "Um, okay then."

"*Yes!*" Rosie clapped her hands together, eyes sparkling. "Could you come to the house after lunch tomorrow?"

Mack bit his lip, plainly torn—I thought I knew what was bothering him.

"How about you come to our place, Ro?" I suggested. "I'll come pick you up and take you back after." At Mum's frown I added, "You can work on something to play for Mum and Derek without them overhearing you practicing."

Mum's frown eased at that and Rosie's on-the-spot bounce reminded me of when she was little and would get excited. "Great! How about two o'clock?"

"Make it three," I said. "That way, the lunch rush will be over before I come and get you." I glanced at Mack. "Does that sound okay to you?"

"Sure," he said, though he still didn't look entirely happy.

And that was how Mack started teaching Rosie guitar.

PROOF

CHAPTER THIRTEEN

October

The next few weeks passed quickly.

Slowly, gradually, Mack was regaining his strength. Rosie too, though she had a steeper hill to climb.

Mack continued to play at the café twice a week but as he got better, I could see he was getting bored, bored of spending too many hours alone, either at the flat or wandering round Porthkennack.

From a domestic point of view, he was an easy flatmate. He did his fair share round the flat, but he wasn't a neat freak, and we got on well. We had a similar sense of humour, liked the same movies and games. I loved having him around—it was like being part of a couple, only without the sex . . .which was, really, the only source of tension between us. On my part anyway—perhaps Mack wasn't even aware it was an issue. He certainly gave no sign. But yeah, for me, I was having trouble hiding how attracted I was to him and I was pretty sure I was regularly slipping up. It felt like he caught me looking at him at least once or twice a day.

When I masturbated, at night or in the shower, it was Mack I'd think about, and that was new. My wank bank had always comprised outlandish fictional situations—I wasn't one for fantasising about people I actually knew or things that could, conceivably happen. But now I found myself remembering those few hours we'd spent at Mack's hotel all those weeks ago. How it had felt to press inside him and feel his body draw me in. How he'd looked beneath me, his long, strong back under my hands as I smoothly fucked him. How it had felt to lay my naked chest down against that milk-white skin and take his shaft in my fist, coaxing his orgasm out of him.

I replayed it in my mind too many times to count.

Midway through October, one of our part-timers handed in her notice. Katie had got herself a childcare qualification the year before and had been searching for a job in a nursery for a while, so it wasn't massive surprise. I was chuffed to bits for her, but I groaned—inwardly of course—when she told me she needed to start straightaway and couldn't work any notice.

"It's a massive pain," I grumbled to Mack at home that night. "I'll need to get someone else quickly because Mum wants to stay at home with Rosie a bit longer."

"I'll do it," he said casually, eyes on the TV screen, thumbs busy on his console. "I've done loads of catering jobs."

I eyed him. "I know. I was thinking about asking you but being on your feet all day isn't a picnic. It's not that long since your surgery."

He glanced up then, tossing the controller aside. "Come on," he scoffed. "It's been nearly eight weeks. I'll be fine. Plus I'm bored and I want to earn some cash. If you don't let me do it, I'll just go and get a job somewhere else."

I knew he wasn't kidding. And the truth was, Katie only did a handful of shifts each week—if I swapped the rota around, I could make sure I was around to do any grunt work when he was working.

"Okay, fine," I said. "On the strict understanding that you promise to tell me the moment you start feeling tired and agree to take regular breaks. Proper sit-down ones. Agreed?"

He rolled his eyes at me, but then nodded and grinned, clearly pleased.

The next morning, it was my turn to open up the café. When I shuffled into the kitchen straight from the shower, a towel slung round my hips, I found Mack already dressed and making tea.

"Oh—uh, morning," I said, jerking to a halt in the doorway, self-conscious about my slight spare tyre. Somehow, for these last few weeks, I'd managed to never be unclothed in front of Mack. Even during our one-night stand, we hadn't exactly been *scrutinising* one another's bodies, so it felt weird to suddenly have my naked chest on show in the far-too-bright morning light.

Mack looked up from the mugs he was dowsing with milk, clocked my state of undress and blinked in surprise. For a long, awkward moment, I stared at him, and he stared at my chest.

At last, he managed to drag his gaze upward again. "Um—I was thinking. If it's okay with you, I'd like to open up with you this morning."

"You don't have to do that," I said stupidly, accepting the cup of tea he held out to me. "You're not meant to start till ten."

"Well, I'd like to—you don't have to pay me for it. I'd just like to scope the place out. See how things work before I get started, you know?"

"Oh, I'll *pay* you," I said hurriedly, horrified at the implication I was being cheap. "It's only that I hadn't planned to start you off with opening up. But sure, if you want to do that, that's fine."

He chuckled. "Hey, I'm just glad to escape another morning of daytime TV."

It was typical of him to wave off the money issue—one of the nicest things about Mack was how easygoing he was. If that'd been me, I'd probably have made a big point of principle about how I wouldn't accept payment for those unsolicited hours and the whole conversation would've become awkward. Not Mack, though.

I took my tea back to the bedroom and quickly dressed in jeans and a polo, examining my belly in the mirror for a bit longer than usual, smoothing my hands down over my torso. When I'd lived in London, I'd been in pretty decent shape thanks to my early morning gym visits and healthy, if expensive, eating habits. I still did some free weights at home so I had reasonable muscle tone—good pecs and arms—but my gut! Jesus, I had to do some cardio and cut out all the carbs and sugar I was eating. If only I was like Mack. God, that man had so much self-control . . . I thought of his long lean torso and swallowed, hard.

I wished it was mere envy I felt when I thought of Mack's body. That had to be better than the unrequited lust that had been riding me since he'd moved in.

With a sigh, I turned away from the mirror.

Mornings were always busy at Dilly's. We opened at eight-thirty on weekdays and our first sit-in customers usually rolled in just after nine—mostly parents who'd dropped off kids at school. Mid-morning brought the pensioners and parents with younger children, followed by the lunchtime rush so there was quite a bit of early prep needed.

That morning, Mack and I got to the café at seven thirty. I showed him round the service counter, coffee machines and till area, explaining our system for orders and payment, then took him into the kitchen and showed him where everything was stored. He picked up the details quickly, his easy grasp of the essentials testament to the many catering jobs he'd had before.

Together, we unloaded stock from the fridge and larder and brought it into the main body of the café, loading up the refrigerated part of the service counter with Clingfilm-wrapped tubs of sandwich fillings, and stocking up the baskets on top of the counter with bread, rolls and pastries.

While Mack filled the coffee grinders with beans, I rolled out some ready-to-bake scone dough Derek had left in the fridge, cut out a couple of dozen rounds and rattled them into the oven. I'd bake another couple of dozen in an hour or so, and probably a third batch just before lunch—the fresher the better with scones. Derek's scones were soft, crumbly and utterly delicious. One of our bestsellers was the "Dilly's special ice-cream afternoon tea"—a warm scone served with clotted cream ice cream and strawberry jam sauce, all homemade.

"We don't make any of our other cakes and pastries," I told Dylan. "Not yet anyway. That's where I want to get to though. Ideally, everything we sell should be homemade."

"Dilly's everything?" Mack teased.

I grinned at him. "Why not? Once we've established the brand, the sky's the limit. I'm looking into getting some of our ice creams into the shops."

Mack raised his eyebrows. "Impressive."

By eight-fifteen, the scones were out of the oven and the café was ready for opening. Mack practiced his barista skills, making us both large coffees, a latte for me and an Americano for him. I hesitated when he passed me the latte—I needed to give up the big milky drinks—but in the end, I caved. It looked too good to pass up, the creamy foam just the right consistency with a fancy little coffee pattern worked into it.

"God, those scones smell amazing," Mack said.

"Wait till you taste them." I opened one up and spread it thickly with butter before handing it to him.

He took a bite. "Oh my *god*," he moaned through a mouthful of pastry.

"I know," I said. "Derek makes them."

Mack swallowed. "Yeah?" He lifted his coffee and took a swig. "By the way, what beans do you use? This is a gorgeous flavour. So nutty."

I told him about our beans—an Italian roast—and for a couple of minutes, we chatted about coffee and the pros and cons of introducing a 'coffee of the month', an alternative flavour for the aficionados amongst our customers. It wasn't till later, when I cleared some packaging away, that I saw he'd chucked the rest of his scone in the bin.

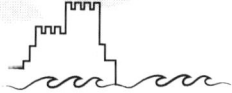

That first morning with Mack went pretty well. He was competent, quiet and hard-working—too hard-working actually—I had to nag at him to take the regular sit-down breaks we'd agreed on. The last thing I wanted was Mack opening up his surgery wound and bleeding out on the floor.

"I'm fine!" he protested as I pushed him into a chair after the lunchtime rush and slid a ham-salad baguette in front of him.

"Eat," I growled, setting a mango and orange smoothie in front of him too. He didn't eat nearly enough fruit or veg and I'd been devising strategies to get more into him over the last few weeks, pulsing up roast veggy pasta sauces and wholesome soups like an overeager parent.

He sighed, but he tucked in, and I couldn't help but smile to see him polish off the lot. He was so lean and spare. I loved how he looked but he could stand to put a little weight on after the rigours of the surgery. And honestly? I suppose I liked taking care of him.

A little while later, the back door to the kitchen opened and a voice called out, "Nathan? Can you give me a hand with this lot, son?"

Derek.

I was making up an order for some customers who'd just sat down.

Mack, who'd finished eating, rose from his chair, lifted his dishes and walked back round the counter. "I can help him," he said.

I shook my head. "No way. No lifting for you. You take over here. A white coffee, a flapjack and a Dilly's ice cream tea." Without giving him a chance to argue, I headed for the kitchen.

Derek did a couple of ice cream deliveries each week from a small unit in the local industrial estate where he made and stored the ice-cream for Dilly's.

"Hi," he said when he saw me. "I've got everything on your order but the mango ripple. The last batch of that didn't set right." He put down the box he was carrying on the worktop.

"All righty," I said. "Let's get this lot in."

I followed him out the back door to the van he'd parked in the lane. We quickly emptied out the ice cream and carried it into the kitchen where I transferred most of it into the chest freezer, leaving out a few of the big ten-litre tubs to replenish the shop freezer: a vanilla, a chocolate chip and a strawberry cheesecake .

"Have you had lunch yet?" I asked hoisting up the tubs and heading for the counter.

"Yeah," he said following me, "But I could murder a coffee if you—oh!" He stopped dead when he saw Mack standing at the till. "Dylan. Hi. I wasn't expecting to see you."

Dylan eyed him coolly. "Didn't Nathan mention I was going to be helping out?" He frowned slightly, and my cheeks warmed. Which was ridiculous—I had nothing to feel embarrassed about.

"I mentioned it to Mum," I told Derek defensively.

He cleared his throat. "Oh, right. She didn't say. Anyway, it's, um, fine—not a problem."

Well, it hadn't been, but now it felt like it was. Mack's face reddened.

I turned to Derek and said firmly, "Mack—I mean, Dylan— agreed to help us out when Katie left. No one's responded to the job advert yet so he's doing us a big favour."

"Oh. I see." Derek looked hunted. He glanced at Mack and said awkwardly, "Nathan and Lorraine sort out the café shifts. I just do the food."

Mack's expression was unfriendly. "Sure."

Christ.

The door chimed then and a couple of little old ladies came in, twittering. As Mack busied himself greeting them, I said wearily to Derek. "Go and sit down. I'll get you that coffee."

I made our drinks, popping a Danish pastry on the tray in case Derek changed his mind about being hungry, and took everything over to his table, settling myself in the chair opposite. He was watching Mack, chatting to the old dears as he took their order.

"He really hates my guts," Derek said hoarsely.

I studied my stepdad. I'd known Derek since I was kid and he'd always been the big man in the room, the loudest, the funniest. I'd never seen him so . . . diminished.

"You need to talk to him," I said, keeping my voice low. "You two clearly have stuff you need to discuss but you avoid him like the plague! What the fuck is that about, Derek? He just donated half his liver to Rosie and you can't even say 'hello' properly?"

Derek slouched over the table, not meeting my eyes. "He doesn't want to talk to me. He couldn't have made that more obvious. I'm respecting his wishes."

"Bullshit," I muttered. "You're being a coward."

"Yeah," he admitted. "I am. But you don't understand, Nathan. Too much damage has been done—there's no coming back from some things."

"What things?"

Derek didn't answer that. Instead he said, "You know, sometimes I feel like I was given a second chance, getting you as a stepson. I fucked things up with Dylan, but everything was so much easier with you. Probably because of Lorraine."

I stilled. I didn't like the thought that I'd been benefitting from Derek's efforts when his own son had been going without. Worse, that him being so good with me might have been a reaction to his guilt over his mistakes with Mack.

"Do you remember when you first told us you were gay?" Derek asked.

I cleared my throat. "Yeah. You said it didn't matter whether I fancied lads or lasses, you and Mum would always love me."

Derek gave a lopsided smile. "You were petrified." His smile faded and suddenly he looked really sad.

"When did you find out Mack was gay?" I asked.

"When he was fifteen."

Fifteen? That must have been on that last visit to Scotland. A bad feeling started in my gut.

I set my mug down. Carefully, I said, "Was that when you went up for his mum's funeral?"

Derek stared down at the uneaten Danish pastry I'd put in front of him, as though fascinated. After a long pause he said, "I got up to Scotland the night before the funeral—he just came out with it. I hadn't seen it coming. I. . . reacted badly." He looked up at me then and his expression was grim. "I felt sure he was far too young to know his own mind about something like that. It came into my head that maybe some older guy had got to him—turned him somehow."

Jesus.

"That's what you said to him?"

"Yeah." Derek put his elbows on the table and dropped his head in his hands.

I was silent, unsure how to react. I couldn't help contrasting the way Derek had received the exact same news from me—only a year later by the sound of it. He'd been so great. I'd thought it was because he'd been in the music industry or something.

"We argued badly that night," Derek said. "I told him I wanted him to come back to Cornwall with me and of course he refused. Then, the next day, we had another fight . . . at the funeral. Dylan pretty much gave me what for. I was angry and humiliated—this was all in front of Tammy's family who all hated me already. In the end, I walked out. Then I got in my car and started driving home." He swallowed. "And I never went back."

I remembered what Mack had told me about that argument. *"I told him I hated him, said I never wanted to see him again."*

I glanced over at Mack behind the counter on the other side of the café. More customers had come in since Derek and I had started talking and Mack was busy serving them, not even looking our way. There was no way he could pick up our murmured conversation but I still felt oddly guilty discussing him when he was right there.

I turned my attention back to Derek. "Was that it, then?" I asked, trying not to show how appalled I was by what he'd disclosed so far. "Did you just stop contacting him?"

"Not right away. I called him a few times over the next few weeks, but he wouldn't speak to me, so I started sending letters instead—he never replied. Mary, Tammy's mother, suggested I back off and give him some time to come around. I suppose if I'm honest, I was glad." Derek gaze was turned downwards, his expression pure self-loathing. "At that point, I let it all slide—the calls, the letters. It was easy to do. I was busy here, and Dylan was being taken care of by Mary and Tom. I always meant to get in touch again, but as time went on, it began to feel . . . impossible."

"Jesus, Derek."

He winced. "I know. I never meant for it to end up like this. But sometimes, life just . . . gets ahead of you." He stared at the table, clearly unable to meet my eyes.

After a while I said, "Does Mum know all this?"

"Some of it. I never told her about what happened that day of the funeral. Or that I'd stopped writing to him." He shifted his gaze back to me, adding almost defiantly, "But I sent all the child support payments. Right up till he was eighteen. I was only ever late with a few at the start, when I first bought this place."

What did he want? A medal? I thought of the years I'd spent shuttling between my parents, a bedroom in both houses, both of them wanting to spend as much time as possible with me. What if one of them had just left me, like Derek had Mack? A regular payment into a bank account wasn't sufficient compensation for that kind of betrayal. That abandonment.

Another thought occurred to me. *How could Mum have let this happen?*

"I can't believe Mum—" I began, but straight away Derek interrupted, pointing a finger at me.

"Hey, your mother is not to blame for *any* of this! For years, I wouldn't even talk to her about Dylan. She tried to get to me to open up, but I wouldn't." He shook his head. Rubbed his hand over his face. "It's all *my* fault, Nathan. I took the easy way out."

Well, I wasn't going to disagree with that.

Instead I said, matter-of-factly, "Okay, but you've got a chance to make it up to him now. And to do that you need to talk to him. Apologise for your mistakes."

He stared at me, seeming genuinely shocked. "I can't," he whispered. "He doesn't want to know. He *hates* me, and I don't blame him."

"You need to at least try," I insisted. "For your sake as much as his."

"But I don't know him anymore," Derek said desperately. "When I last saw him, he came up to here"—he indicated just above his shoulder— "Now he's taller than me, a fully grown man. And he's made it crystal clear he doesn't want to discuss the past with me. How am I supposed to make him listen?"

I glared at him, as annoyed by his excuses as I was dismayed. Derek wasn't usually the sort to give up easily but he seemed to want to throw in the towel on this without even trying. The unfairness of that, to Mack, burned in me.

"What about what he did for Rosie?" I hissed, trying to keep my voice down. "Don't you think you owe it him to swallow your pride, apologise for giving up on him and thank him for saving your daughter's life?"

Derek went white. He stared at me in silence, mouth clamped shut, a muscle working in his cheek. I had the weirdest sense he was only barely holding back tears, but that couldn't be right. Derek never cried and rarely showed any real emotion. He and Mack were alike in that respect.

When he said nothing, I pushed my chair back and stood. "You know this might be the only opportunity you get to put this thing with Mack right. You shouldn't waste that chance."

CHAPTER
FOURTEEN

Mack and I closed up the café just after five and headed back to the flat. He made us a brew and we watched a crappy quiz show, then I headed into the kitchen to make us some dinner. I was chopping onions for a stir fry when he ambled in.

"Want a hand?"

"Nah," I said. "This won't take long."

He didn't leave though. Instead, he leaned against the counter, watching me work, saying nothing. I smiled at him but stayed silent, waiting for him to speak. I was learning to give him space to do that.

Eventually he said, "You and Derek seemed to be having a deep and meaningful chat earlier."

Ah.

I kept my gaze fixed on the red pepper I was slicing into strips. "Yeah, I suppose we were."

Silence. Then, warily, "Was it about me?"

"Maybe."

I expected him to demand I tell him exactly what we'd been talking about then, but he didn't. He frowned. "Listen, don't worry about me and Derek. It's not your problem, okay?"

I put the knife down and turned to look at him properly. His expression was guarded and he had his arms crossed over his chest, hugging himself. I found myself remembering that first night again. How he'd asked me to hold him. Did anyone else ever hold Mack? Were his grandparents affectionate in that way? Any of his boyfriends?

Had he even had boyfriends in that way, or had he just fucked around? He'd never mentioned anyone significant to me.

I clenched my hands by my sides to stop myself reaching for him.

"He feels bad, you know? About the past."

Mack gave a short, astonished laugh. "You don't really believe that, do you? My dad's a dick, Nathan. He wanted nothing to do with me when I was kid. Don't go getting ideas into your head about fixing us."

I took a deep breath. "I totally understand why you feel he didn't care about you, I *do*, but I also don't think that's necessarily true. Maybe if you two talked—"

"Jesus, will you *take a hint?*" he yelled, eyes blazing. "I don't want you to get involved in this! The whole world is not your fucking responsibility!"

Stung, I snapped back, "Okay, understood! I'll stay out of your business. I just wanted you to know someone fucking cares. Excuse me for giving a shit." I turned away and picked up my knife again, grabbing the pepper, but as annoyed as I was, I failed to pay proper attention and sliced into my index finger.

"Fuck!" I cursed, dropping the knife and crossing to the sink, yanking on the tap and sticking my hand under. The cold water sluiced away the blood as I examined the cut.

"Jesus, are you okay?" Mack asked, coming up behind me. He stuck his head over my shoulder. "You're bleeding a lot."

I peered at the cut. "It doesn't look too bad. Can you get me a plaster? There's a box in one of those drawers."

While Mack rifled through the drawers, I pressed on the cut with my thumb to stop the bleeding. He found a dog-eared box of plasters which he upended onto the counter, shuffling through them to find one the right size.

"Show me your finger." He ripped the outer packaging of a plaster open.

"Just give it here," I said, holding out my other hand. "I can do it."

"Calm down, Mr. Control Freak. I'm not going to mess up. Show me your finger."

Huffing a little, I held out my hand, gingerly lifting my thumb. The bleeding had slowed, revealing a cut that was small but deep. Mack carefully laid the white gauzy bit over the cut and wrapped the sticky ends neatly round my finger tip.

"There," he said, and his voice was strangely husky.

I glanced up.

I think I meant to say thank you. Say it and step away and go back to chopping vegetables. But Mack's face was closer than I'd expected it to be, and his dark gaze was on me, his expression strangely tender. Unguarded.

And somehow it seemed like a good idea to kiss him.

It was a brief kiss. Short and warm and—for me—heart-stopping. Till he pulled back, simultaneously pushing at my shoulder with one hand to make sure we broke apart.

Shit, I'd read him wrong.

My stomach turned over sickeningly and I opened my eyes reluctantly, expecting to see regret, maybe even horror on his face. Instead, to my surprise, I found him gazing at me questioningly. No, more than questioningly. Flirtatiously, with one eyebrow raised and an amused look that said *Are you thinking what I'm thinking?*

I whispered, "This could really complicate things."

He smiled. "Only if we let it—and I don't intend to. Do you?"

I just stared at him helplessly and he moved in closer, pressing his hips against mine. His already hard cock prodded mine and I couldn't suppress a groan.

"There's no reason we can't just have some fun," he said huskily. "We're both grown-ups. I fancy you, and I think you fancy me . . ."

Fucking understatement of the year.

"I do," I agreed, sighing. "Kind of a lot. Have I been really obvious?"

His eyes widened as though my words had taken him aback. "Not at all."

For a long moment, we stared at each other, then I said, knowing it was a terrible idea. "Do you want to come to my room?"

His answering smile was slow.

Just like on that first night, Mack shed his clothes quickly, not waiting for me to begin. He discarded his stuff on the floor of my bedroom and paced towards me, loose-limbed and lean. I envied his ease with his nudity. For my part, I was glad of the closed blinds and the low evening light.

My gaze snagged on the surgery scar, and I reached out, tentative, barely grazing the purplish edges with my fingertips.

I said, "Are you sure you'll be okay with—", only to break off at Mack's chuckle. When I glanced up, his dark eyes were dancing with wicked amusement.

"I'm in full working order," he assured me with a grin. "I've experimented."

The image of Mack 'experimenting' as he lay naked on the bed in my spare room made my mouth dry up.

"Okay," I said hoarsely. I stepped closer to him and sought his mouth again. He didn't reject me but his answering kiss was a mere brush of his lips before he started nibbling his way down my throat.

It felt too good to complain about the loss of his lips on mine. Instead I let my head go back, encouraging him, while he fumbled with the button at the neck of my polo shirt, then drew it over my head.

The stab of embarrassment that hit me whenever I first got undressed melted away at the expression on his face. It was obvious he liked what he saw. He ran his hands up my sides, dark eyes heavy-lidded as they greedily took me in.

"You're so fuckin' gorgeous," he muttered, his Scottish accent more pronounced than usual. He bent his head to kiss my shoulder while he played with my nipples, brushing them with his thumbs then pinching them tightly, making me moan and my cock jump.

"Gotta taste your cock," he said, lowering himself to his knees. He kissed my belly as he started working my jeans open, tonguing my belly button, and rubbing his cheek against the slight softness there.

I stroked his head, tunneling my fingers gently through his hair. I loved the colour of it, as dark as brown gets before it's officially black, and the silky feel of it, cool against my fingers. I remembered how much he'd liked me tugging on it that first night and tangled my fingers in it again, just enough to hint at what he wanted. He moaned in answer and yanked my fly open, carefully working my cock free before taking me down his throat.

"*Fuck*," I groaned. "That's so good."

He sucked me eagerly, expertly. I could've come in about thirty seconds with all that wet heat and perfect clasping pressure on my swollen dick but I didn't want this finishing any time soon, so instead I tugged at his hair. He came off me with *pop*, sitting back on his heels to gaze up at me with a molten, dazed expression.

"Let me do you too," I pleaded. "We can sixty-nine."

"Okay," he murmured, clambering to his feet.

I shed my jeans *en route* to the bed, my shyness burned away by the lustful way he looked at me. Mack laid himself down with his head at the pillow end, so I laid down the other way and reached for him.

I fucking loved sixty-nining—I could do it for ages, edging my partner over and over—and it seemed Mack liked it too, if his eagerness was anything to go by. He swallowed my dick down to the root, his slick tongue working my shaft, before I had even tasted him. I arched against his mouth for a long, blissful moment before galvanising myself into action, sliding my fingers over his sharp hipbones then curving my hands over his buttocks to pull him closer to me.

He smelled amazing, clean and musky at once. I was conscious of him as a warm, healthy male animal and it felt good—right—to push my cheek against his shaft and turn my face to lick the silky skin.

I licked him without using my hands, without taking him into my mouth yet, painting every millimetre of his shaft with my tongue, till he was groaning around my own dick, his lips losing suction as he reacted to my attentions. Only for a second, though, and then he was sucking me desperately again.

I moved off his cock, dipping my head further down to explore the tight wrinkled sac that encased his balls with my tongue, urging his legs to part. He shifted obediently to give me more access, gasping as I tongued and sucked the tender spheres of his testicles, gently mouthing then releasing them. He gasped as I moved lower still, nibbling my way slowly down, past the silken patch of his perineum, till I found the very edge of his entrance, pink and tight and mostly obscured from view, but close enough to just touch with the tip of my tongue, if I stretched.

At that first glancing touch of my tongue to his rim, he gave a cry that was part protest, part astonishment, part surrender and I grunted with satisfaction at his reaction, pushing his thighs wider to open him up to me.

I lifted my head, saying hoarsely, "Keep sucking my dick," before dipping back down to my own task.

He resumed blowing me, but already his technique was growing sloppy as I distracted with him with the opening bars of what I'd now decided was going to be the best rimming he'd ever had.

I don't know how long we lasted in the end, him sucking me in a desperate messy way that made me feel like a fucking king while I dismantled his sanity with a relentless rim-job that had him sobbing and begging around my dick. At last though, he pulled off me to gasp, "Gonna come—can't hold off."

I retreated and finally gave him the prize I'd promised him at the beginning, taking his delicious cock into my mouth, while sliding two fingers into now soft and relaxed hole.

He cried out and started coming almost immediately, coating the back of my throat with a spray of salt like a breaking wave. With a groan of gratitude, I let myself go over an instant later, giving up the iron control I'd been exerting to keep my pleasure in check, surrendering to the wrenching, pulsing orgasm Mack dragged out of my guts with his incredible mouth.

Afterwards, Mack flopped to his back, gasping, "Fuckin' hell." And I burst out laughing, giddy with the joy of sexual release. A moment later he joined in, and we lay there, head-to-crotch, splatters of semen drying on us as we laughed breathlessly at nothing in particular. It felt like relief and amusement and happiness all wrapped together, a reaction, maybe, to the suppressed sexual tension between us finding its ease.

Eventually, I sat up, turned myself the right way round and looked down at him.

"Hey," I said, offering a crooked smile.

He smiled back, if a little guardedly. "Hey."

What I really wanted, in that moment, was to lie down beside him and pull him into my arms, but I didn't feel like I could. Without saying or doing anything, Mack had somehow made himself remote.

Slowly, he sat up, managing to create some mattress space between us as he did so.

When he met my gaze, his smile was broad but curiously distant. "God, I needed that," he said, then chuckled. "Thanks, man."

Like I'd scratched an itch for him.

My heart sank. Fuck, I'd known as soon as he'd suggested this that it wasn't a good idea.

Well, it wasn't Mack's fault that I wasn't into casual hook-ups. Of the two of us, I was the unusual one, probably.

I dropped my gaze, not trusting myself to speak. What was I supposed to say, after all? *You're welcome?*

He didn't seem to notice my lack of reaction, was too busy getting up and grabbing his boxers from the floor, donning them quickly.

"Christ, I'm starving," he announced. "How about I finish making dinner?"

"I'll do it," I said automatically, getting to my feet. "I've already started. I only need to finish chop—"

"Nathan," he interrupted, his tone exasperated. "Can you just let me do *something*? For once?"

My head jerked up and I looked at him, astonished. "What?"

He gave a hard sigh. "You don't have to do everything, all the time."

"What do you mean" I sounded defensive now. "I don't."

"Yeah, you do. You take care of everything, for everyone. But I don't need you to do that for me. I know it's important for you to—" He stopped, pressing his lips together.

My heart was pounding. "To what?" I bit out. "What do you think is important to me?"

He eyed me for a long moment. "You like to be needed—and that's fine. Your mum, Rosie, my dad, they all need you. Personally, I think they expect too much of you sometimes, but if you're all right with it . . ." He shrugged, then added, "But not me, okay? I don't need that. I can do my fair share."

I didn't know what to say. I just stared at him. What was he saying, that I had some kind of martyr complex? Or worse, that I got people to love me by making them feel beholden to me? My cheeks were suddenly hot. I must be bright red. I felt insulted and stupid and thoroughly rejected.

Mack's hard expression crumbled at whatever he saw on my face. "I'm sorry," he said. "I shouldn't have said that. It's none of my business how you deal with your family."

Your family.

Not his. Not even ours.

Yours.

At that instant, I just felt incredibly . . . sad. Still angry, still hurt, but sad more than anything else. And I couldn't think of a thing to say. What was the point is saying *They're your family too*—he obviously didn't see it like that.

I turned away, hiding my face from him. "I could do with a shower—if the offer to finish dinner's still on the table, I won't stop you."

"Okay, good." He sounded relieved. "Chicken stir fry, right?"

"Yeah. Chicken's in the fridge. There's rice in the cupboard or noodles if you prefer."

"Coming right up," he said, positively cheerful now. "I hope you like it spicy!"

CHAPTER
FIFTEEN

I need you back; I want you back
The one I thought loved me so bad
You looked at me like I could be
The best guy that you ever had
Like someday soon I'd hang the moon
Right there amongst the stars that glow
But now it seems I killed those dreams
And you're packing up your stuff so you can go . . .
(Repeat chorus)
Christmas Stocking by The Sandy Coves, 1989

November

I suppose I'd hoped things would change between me and Mack after that night, but somehow they just went back to how they'd been before. The next day, Mack made no mention of us having sex and I, nervous of spooking him, followed his lead. And so it went, for the next couple of weeks.

I put up the Hallowe'en decorations. Bought in orange- and green-iced cupcakes. Took the decorations down again. And suddenly it was November. Cold and grey and pitch dark by the time I closed up the café each night. Mack and I worked our shifts together during the day and passed our evenings in the same amicable way we'd done before. Mack played guitar a lot which was fine with me. I liked listening to him while I read or caught up on paperwork.

On the Friday after Hallowe'en, Rosie came over for her guitar lesson. As usual, she banished me from the room—she hated being watched—so I sat in the kitchen with my laptop. I could hear the soft rumble of Rosie and Mack's voices and their frequent laughter in between the snatches of music. It made me smile and feel envious at the same time.

Who was it I was envious of? Both of them maybe. Rosie and Mack were more alike than me and Rosie. My sister was a chatterbox, like Mum, but deep down, she had the same laid-back attitude to life that Mack had—and that they both seemed to have inherited from Derek.

Whilst that easy attitude had been a major factor in Dilly's getting into such a mess, I had to admit it had its upsides. It was clear that Rosie found Mack easy to be around. As for Mack, he showed a soft side when he was with her that was noticeably absent the rest of the time, his expression losing some of its innate wariness in her presence.

When the lesson was over, Rosie poked her head round the kitchen door.

"Hey," she said. "I'm off."

I shut my laptop. "I'll walk you back."

"No need. Mack's coming. Not that I need either of you." She made a face.

"Sorry but you know the rules." Mum wasn't ready to let Rosie walk around on her own yet. It was progress that she wasn't insisting on driving her here and picking her up.

She sighed heavily, all put upon.

"Anyway," I said, getting off my school and opening my arms. "Gimme a hug before you go. I need one."

She rolled her eyes, but she was smiling as she came closer and let me wrap her up, giving a contented little sigh against my chest.

We were still hugging a couple of minutes later when Mack walked into the kitchen, saying, "Are we going then, Ro?"

He stopped dead when he saw us, staring at us as though we were aliens.

"We're having a hug," I explained.

"Oh."

Rosie broke out of my embrace and moved towards him. "Your turn," she said, opening her arms.

He actually looked scared. I suppose it was funny in a way, but it made my chest ache watching as he raised his arms and stepped back as though to get away from her. It did him no good anyway—she just moved into his space and put her arms round his waist, squeezing him hard. He winced a little—God, his poor scar—then, after a moment, he patted her back awkwardly and sent me a look that seemed to say, *Am I doing this right?* I grinned at him teasingly, as though I really was amused by his predicament but in truth, my heart felt all twisted up. His unfamiliarity with simple affection tore at me. Not that he'd want my pity. He'd be mortified if he could read my thoughts.

Eventually Rosie let him go and they headed back to Mum's. When Mack got back, I had a big bowl of salty popcorn and drinks waiting—beer for me, Coke for Mack.

"I thought we could watch a movie." I was already searching options, clicking through a menu of recent releases, most of which we'd seen already. "I don't fancy any of these."

Mack settled on the couch beside me and reached for the popcorn. "How about we watch something different for a change?" he suggested. "An independent film maybe? If I have to watch another superhero movie I'm going to start thinking *I'm* a superhero."

It was on the tip of my tongue to answer that we could just watch some porn instead, but I knew that wasn't a smart suggestion. Instead, I tossed him the remote. "Pick whatever you like. Just no gay tragedies please."

He laughed. "No *Brokeback Mountain*, got it."

He flicked through the menus for so long I zoned out. Finally, though, he stopped. "Oh, I heard this was good. Let's give it a try."

"It's Spanish," I whined. "I'm too tired to read the subtitles."

"Oh, give it a go," he groused. "I've watched practically every Marvel movie with you over the last few weeks. It's the least you can do."

"Movie snob," I sighed, reaching for another beer. "Fine. Put it on."

We'd got into the habit of switching off the main lights when we watched movies at night, sitting in the dark with my big plasma screen lit up like a mini cinema. Now, as the opening titles played, I stole a glance at Mack, watching the play of the flickering lights and colours on his face, quickly averting my gaze when he looked my way.

There were a lot of characters in the movie. A complicated plot too, everyone talking in rapid Spanish. Despite my whinging, it was a lot better than I'd thought it would be and I was reluctantly drawn in, almost forgetting that Mack was sitting beside me . . . until the sex scene started.

The hero stripped his clothes off—he was a beautiful man, his naked body smooth and golden, his eyes burning with emotion as he approached the heroine. The camera kissed his body, lingering over every perfect line, pausing on his perfect, sculpted back then drifting down to take in his taut arse and long legs.

"Christ, that's hot," Mack muttered beside me.

"Yeah." I shifted in my seat to ease the pressure at my crotch

"He looks a bit like you," Mack added without taking his eyes off the screen, making me glance at him in astonishment.

"Maybe if I lost two stone," I scoffed.

He turned to me, frowning. "Don't do that."

"Do what?"

"Put yourself down like that. I don't know why you do it—you must know you're gorgeous."

Pleasure flooded me and for a moment I couldn't look away from his penetrating gaze. For some reason, though, my stupid mouth kept running on. "Oh, come on, I need to lose a stone. My stomach . . ." I touched my belly, self-conscious.

Mack stared at me for a couple of beats, then he said firmly, "Take your shirt off."

"What?"

"Take your shirt off. Let me see."

My mouth went dry but I did as he said, reaching for the hem of my t-shirt and drawing it slowly over my head. My cheeks were warm by the time it came off, my stomach knotting with mingled desire and embarrassment. In the background, the movie played on, but neither of us were watching anymore.

I dropped my T-shirt on the floor and sat back, letting Mack look me over, He gazed at my torso, his eyes tracking me all over. I couldn't breathe as I withstood his scrutiny. At length, he said quietly, "How can you think there's anything wrong with your body? You're amazing."

Jesus.

I cleared my throat awkwardly. My cock had filled as his gaze had roved over me, though it wasn't yet obvious with the loose joggers I was wearing, and the way I was sitting. "I used to be leaner," I added. The tightness in my my voice betrayed my tension. "My diet's gone downhill though and I don't exercise as much as I used to."

"I think you look great," he murmured, gaze moving again, almost hungrily. "You have great shoulders and for someone who claims he doesn't exercise enough your muscle tone is really good." He licked his lips and my cock pulsed.

I stroked my hand over my belly. Swallowed. "I just need to lose some of this."

He glanced back at my face then and gave me a wry, one-sided grin. "Don't be a spoilsport. I like a little meat on a guy's bones."

We stared at each other in silence. Despite his light-hearted words, the mood between us had subtly changed. In the background, the characters on screen panted and kissed, muttering to each other in passionate Spanish as violins soared.

Softly, Mack said, "Can I touch you?"

My heart was banging in my chest. "Okay," I breathed.

He surprised me by going straight to his knees on the floor, moving his lean body into the space between my open legs. My dick throbbed as I gazed at him, waiting, wanting.

Slowly he reached out, sliding his warm palms up over my belly, past my ribs and my pecs, curving his hands over my shoulders, his touch gradually growing bolder and firmer, his gaze concentrated on me.

I watched him, fascinated by the gleam of lust in his eyes as he learned every inch of my body. Keeping my breathing shallow and my hands still, I let him do just as he wanted, afraid to make a sound in case I broke the strange spell between us. I never wanted this to end. I loved having his hands on me. His dark, melting gaze on me.

I held my breath as he leaned forward and kissed my stomach, turning his face to rub his cheek into the slight softness after, his closed eyes and moan of pleasure telling me just how much he liked this. He pressed little kisses against my skin as he moved higher and higher, his lips tracing over my ribs, teeth catching on one small, tight nipple, making me gasp. Eventually, he clambered right up onto the couch again, straddling my thighs with his own, and grazing his teeth up my throat till he reached my ear.

"I think your body's fucking perfect," he breathed.

I turned my head so we were eye to eye. His gaze glittered with lust and I knew mine probably did too.

I whispered, "Let me kiss you."

He seemed puzzled. "Why?"

I smiled at that. At his confusion. "Because I want to. How come you never let me?"

"I let you," he protested. "The other day, in your room. Before we blew each other."

"Not really," I said, smiling to take the sting out of it. "Not the way I want to."

He hesitated.

"Come on. Please. You might like it."

He sighed. "Okay then."

I took his face in my hands and guided his lips to mine, gazing at him the whole time, till I settled my mouth over his. I didn't go in with my tongue, not yet, but alternated tiny suckling pulls and nibbles at his lips with glancing sweeps of the very tip of my tongue that made his breath catch. And all the while I was arching my body against his and pushing my hips up, getting us both so hot that, in the end, it wasn't me but Mack who parted his lips and thrust his tongue right into my mouth, deepening the kiss the way I wanted.

I moaned with satisfaction, tunnelling my fingers into the hair at the back of his neck as I opened to him, letting him take whatever he wanted from me. And God, did he take. He pinned me to the back of the sofa with his wiry body and his hands got busy shoving down my joggers as he tongue-fucked my mouth.

And I just sat there, uncharacteristically passive, letting him do whatever he wanted to me, helplessly turned-on by his apparent need for me. I gasped into his mouth when his questing fingers grazed my cock and he began to draw it out of my joggers. And then he was pressing it against his own bare dick, and beginning a rhythmic stroking.

For a guy who wouldn't kiss me before, he was suddenly very into it, lips mauling mine, tongue in my mouth. But as his hand sped up on our dicks, he tore his mouth away, pressing his forehead against mine and closing his eyes as he worked us together.

"Nathan," he moaned. "Fuck, what you do to me."

My heart swelled with gratitude at his words. I was amazed I did anything to him, but right now, he did seem to like me—

—and *fuck* but I liked him.

In fact, going by the ache that spread in my chest as I watched him coming, I liked him way too much.

After that night, there was no more *will-we-won't-we?* We fell into the habit of sleeping together—or rather, fucking—most nights. Mack never stayed over in my bed though.

We didn't talk about it either. Mack made it pretty clear, pretty quick that he wasn't comfortable acknowledging what we were doing too explicitly. Whenever I said anything—even if just to ask him if he wanted me to suck his dick—he'd shut me up with his mouth.

Which was something of an incentive to ask him a lot.

His aversion to kissing seemed to have faded too—at least, he didn't seem to mind the tongue-fucking sort of kisses we'd shared that night on the sofa. He still didn't seem to like the more tender variety though, making sure to quickly sexualise any embraces we shared.

Looking back, I'm amazed that what was going on between us wasn't obvious to everyone else. We couldn't get enough of one another at that point. We spent every night holed up in the flat together, fucking, and whenever we were working together in the café, I spent the whole shift eyeing him.

And yet, we didn't talk about any of it. Not what was happening between us. Not my fear that Mack was just going to up and leave one day without warning.

Not the fact that I was falling for him, hard.

I'd been in relationships and I liked being part of a couple. Liked having someone of my own. My partners had always seemed to feel the same way.

As those first weeks with Mack—in whatever this thing between us was—passed, I found myself really thinking about those previous relationships. I realised that all my boyfriends had told me they loved me before I'd returned the sentiment. That I'd never had to face up to the possibility of rejection when I'd told a guy I loved him. What's more, I'd always been the one to end things and while a couple of those break-ups had made me unhappy for a while, not one of them had torn me apart.

Not one.

What was it Gav had said? That I'd "fallen into" those relationships? At the time, I'd been oddly offended by that accusation but now I thought that maybe he'd been onto something. All my old boyfriends had had one thing in common—they were predictable. They gave me certainty and comfort, if not much excitement.

With Mack, things were different. Frankly, he didn't seem to want anything from me but my dick. I must admit, it was difficult to resent him for that when he was taking me to the back of his throat, but the rest of time I felt . . . I don't know, unsettled. Definitely uncertain. For the first time in my life, *I* was the one with feelings to confess first. Feelings that I was pretty sure weren't returned. Feelings that I suspected would have Mack running out the door like a hare if I gave voice to them.

The trouble was, I wasn't the kind of man to keep my emotions locked down and trying to stay silent took its toll. Mum might not have noticed what was going on between Mack and me, but she noticed that much.

"Are you not sleeping?" she asked one Wednesday evening. Mack was playing in the café and the place was full of customers. Rosie had snagged a table near him with two of her friends while Mum and I shared our usual table next to the counter.

"I'm fine," I said, adding to distract her, "I'm just a bit nervous—Derek and I have that meeting with Fletchers' Delis next Friday."

Mum glanced at me sharply. "What time?"

"Ten—but it's in Truro so we'll have to drive down."

Mum sighed. "Derek won't be able to make it, love. We've got an appointment at the hospital with Rosie that day. He's got to be there."

I was surprised by the sting of resentment that needled my gut at that. I didn't begrudge Rosie having Derek at her appointment—I really didn't. But more than ever these days, it seemed like I was running Dilly's single-handedly. Like Mum and Derek were employees who thought all they needed to do was pitch up for the odd shift or make a few batches of Raspberry Ripple.

"I think they expect too much of you sometimes..."

"Nathan?"

I met Mum's concerned gaze.

"Are you okay?"

I debated saying something then ... but I couldn't do it. Mum had had so much to contend with lately, and she needed to concentrate on Rosie right now. She didn't need me getting on her case about the fucking café. I felt like a dick that it even crossed my mind that she should.

"Yeah, of course," I said quickly, adding in a blatant change of subject, "So, how do you feel about Rosie's appointment on Friday?"

Mum smiled tentatively. "I don't want to get my hopes up, but she's been so much better these last two weeks. I feel like we've turned a corner." She babbled on happily about the minutiae of how Rosie had been, what she'd been eating and drinking and how much she'd slept. I smiled and nodded, half-listening to her and half to Mack who was singing my favourite of the songs he played, *Carrickfergus*. I loved that song. Loved the way his low voice stroked the words and the sad, sweet tune.

He did one more number after that one, a stripped-back country song, then wound up for the night. The customers began to depart and I got busy clearing tables. Mum started helping but Rosie was tired so I shooed them off, assuring them that Mack and I would close up.

The next time I glanced over at Mack, all the customers had gone except one guy, dark-haired and nice-looking, who was chatting to him. I recognised the guy but couldn't quite place him. The stab of jealousy that went through me seeing them together was ... new. I'd never been the jealous type but when the guy clasped Mack's bicep with one hand and grinned at him, I was seized by an uncharacteristic desire to walk over there and, I don't know, stake my claim or something.

Shaking my head at my stupid thoughts, I turned away, making myself focus on the tedious business of closing up. I glanced up at the chime of the doorbell a few minutes later. Mack was locking the door. Finally, we were alone.

When he turned to face me, his expression was uncertain.

"What's up?" I asked.

He blinked. "What? Oh, nothing." He crossed the floor and joined me at the counter. Began wiping down the coffee machine.

"Who was that guy you were talking to?" I asked, careful to keep my voice relaxed.

"Don? He organizes the folk night at the Sea Bell. He said he liked what I did." He cleared his throat. "He offered me a slot actually."

"Really? That's great!"

Mack frowned. "I don't know. I said I'd do it, but I'm not sure it's worth it."

"Why not? You love to play—getting paid for doing what you love sounds like a no-brainer to me." I grinned but he didn't return my smile, concentrating instead on cleaning the stubborn milk residue off the steamer wands.

"There's probably not much point," he said after a while, sending a blast of steam out of one wand before turning his attention to the second one. "He said he's looking for a regular and I'll be heading off soon."

My stomach sank. "Not that soon." My voice came out way more relaxed than I felt. "Your final scan's not for another few weeks."

He shrugged. "I feel fine."

I put my hand on his arm, pulling him round so he had to face me. "Hey," I said. "You can't leave till after that scan. They've got to check your liver's growing back properly—that's not something you can just skip."

He sighed, heavy. "Yeah. I know."

His reluctance to stay in Porthkennack was painful, but I covered up my disappointment with a smile. "So . . . are you going to agree to play at the Sea Bell? I think you should."

His mouth quirked in a lopsided smile. "Yeah, I suppose. I might as well get a couple of gigs out of this stay before I leave."

I wanted to ask him what would happen after that, when he decided it was time to go. I wanted to demand to know if he'd tell me he was leaving or if he'd just get up one morning and decide he was done.

If he'd even say goodbye.

But I didn't ask any of those things. Instead, I took the tubs of sandwich filling through to the kitchen and started stacking them in the fridge.

PROOF

CHAPTER SIXTEEN

On Friday mornings, Denise—a totally unflappable sixty year old who used to run a burger van—opened up the café. Since she could run the place with one hand tied behind her back, I only had to go in at lunchtime. Even then, I usually felt like I was getting under her feet.

Thanks to Denise's efficiency, I tended to have a bit of a lie-in on Friday mornings, so when Mack slouched into the kitchen early one Friday morning to find me up and dressed with my laptop already open at the kitchen table, he seemed surprised.

"Is Denise sick?" he asked as he poured himself a coffee from the pot I'd made.

I shook my head. "No, I've got that meeting in Truro—the one with deli people."

He leaned against the worktop, all sleep-rumpled and appealing, "Oh, right. Is Derek picking you up?"

"Hmm? Oh, no. He's not coming now. Rosie's got a hospital appointment."

Mack frowned. "I see." He paused, then added, "Are you okay going on your own?"

I shrugged. "I'll cope—it's not like I have a choice."

I turned my eyes back to my keyboard but could feel his gaze on me. After a bit, he said, his tone hesitant, "I can come with you—if you'd like a bit of moral support?"

I glanced up, opening my mouth to say no, it was fine, I could manage.

But then I stopped myself and really thought about it.

The truth was, my stomach was knotted with nerves and I felt totally out of my depth.

And actually, it would be nice to have someone there to chat to me on the way so I didn't spend the journey fruitlessly obsessing over what to say. And to post-mortem with on the way back.

"Okay. That would be great."

His smile was oddly sweet and I felt warmth bloom in my chest.

"Can I have ten minutes to shower and change?" he asked.

"Better than that. You can have fifteen," I said.

"In that case, I'll shave as well, if you like."

"Nah, let's rock the entrepreneurial hipster look. A clean shirt'll do."

He winked at me. "Done."

The meeting went well. Really well.

Angie Fletcher was former accountant and her husband Dave had been a wine merchant. They'd left London for the South West eighteen years before to set up their first delicatessen, with a focus on local produce. Since then, they'd grown the business gradually, concentrating on small but well-to-do towns with plenty of tourist trade.

As soon as we arrived, they confessed how excited they were by the plans I'd outlined in my emails and it was plain they had a genuine passion for local independent producers. They showed us several other local product lines they stocked that had managed break into national retailers.

After a quick tour of the deli, Dave led us up to the flat above the main shop and into the kitchen. He made pot of coffee while the rest of us sat down round the kitchen table and I got out the papers I'd brought.

"Are these the packaging ideas?" Angie asked, reaching for a plastic folder. She flicked past the generic two-litre tubs Derek preferred with their old-fashioned designs, but paused at the cute half-litre cartons I'd proposed.

"I *love* this design," Angie said, pointing to my own favourite, a small pint-size carton with strong banded colours and a simple logo:

shocking pink and acid green for our Rhubarb Ripple, sable brown and vivid orange for Chocolate Orange Fondant.

"Our customers aren't looking to fill their freezers with bargains," Angie went on. "They want something special and they'll usually be eating it that night. They don't mind paying a bit over the odds for it, especially if it's unusual and luxurious, and this screams unusual and luxurious."

The Fletchers couldn't have been more encouraging and generous with their time—we ended up spending two hours with them and left with screeds of notes of their suggestions and a promise they'd pop in to the café the next time they were passing Porthkennack to see how things were going and have a taste test.

I couldn't stop smiling when we left.

"I can't believe how well that went," I said to Mack when got back in the car. "They seemed genuinely interested, didn't you think?"

Mack pulled smoothly out of the tiny parking space he'd managed to cram us into earlier. "Yes, thanks to you. You were great," he said. "They couldn't help but get caught up in your enthusiasm." When he glanced at me, his eyes were warm. "I got pretty caught up in it myself."

I flushed with pleasure. "Thanks for coming," I said. "It really helped, having you there. I was so nervous."

"You didn't seem nervous," Mack assured me. "No one would have known."

"*You* knew. You knew this morning, didn't you?"

"You had a wee bit of a rabbit-in-the-headlights look to you," he admitted, and I laughed.

"I thought I was hiding it better than that."

"Yeah, but I've got the measure of you now. I'm beginning to recognise the signs of when you're stressed."

"Oh yeah?" I said, amused. "Like what."

"You get this distracted expression," he said. "And you fiddle with your earlobe."

I laughed, "Do I? I've never noticed that."

"Yup," he assured me.

"You're quite observant, aren't you?"

He shrugged. "Sometimes. Probably comes from moving around so much. You get used to sizing people up quickly when you're always starting somewhere new."

"Do you never fancy . . . *not* moving on to a new place?"

He went very quiet. He was quiet so long, I thought he wasn't going to answer at all. Then he said, "Sometimes. But when it comes down to it, I usually get to a point when I realise I don't have anything to stay for."

His words felt like a gut punch.

I wondered when he'd reach that point with Porthkennack.

That evening, we strolled round to the house to find out how Rosie's hospital appointment had gone. When we got there, Mum was high as a kite. She'd opened a bottle of Prosecco and the remains of a Chinese takeaway were scattered on the coffee table. Derek was apparently at the pub with his mate.

"Are we celebrating?" I asked carefully. Rosie was sitting in her usual spot, headphones in place, though she tore them off when she saw Mack and got up to greet him, hugging him tight. I'd noticed that Mack seemed to be getting more comfortable with her hugs lately.

"It went really well," Mum said, her voice cracking a little with emotion. "The doctor said she's doing brilliantly."

Rosie grinned, letting go of Mack to hug me too, before dragging Mack over the sofa and pulling out her guitar. Within a couple of minutes, they were absorbed, leaving Mum and me to talk.

She gave me the lowdown on the appointment, talking me through everything the doctor had said and his final assurance that Rosie was recovering well.

"That's brilliant," I said.

"Isn't it?" Mum said, her expression a little misty. "Just look at her: she's like a new person."

And she was. I don't think any of us had realised how badly Rosie had been affected by her condition until after the transplant. Seeing her well again, I was reminded of what a livewire she'd been when she was younger and how much she'd changed when she'd been ill.

I watched her and Mack, fascinated. With Rosie, he was different than he was with everyone else. More open, though in a painfully cautious way. Like always, I felt a weird mix of emotions seeing them together. My heart ached to see the wariness in Mack—that fear of letting others in—but the ache was lightened by fond amusement as I witnessed Rosie trampling all over his careful fences and Mack trying to deal with her oblivious trespassing. To my shame, there was still an element of envy in there, that Rosie could reach a part of Mack—hell, say it, his *heart*—that I couldn't touch.

Mum must have seen something of my thoughts on my face, though she misinterpreted them.

"I know it's hard to see the way Rosie is with Dylan," she murmured beside me. "But it doesn't mean she loves you any less. You'll always be her big brother. It's just that Dylan's . . . well, he's new and exciting."

No arguments from me on that front.

I wondered what Mum would think if she knew that it was the tender, almost confused looks Mack was giving Rosie that I coveted. Her ability to step over that invisible line of his without being pushed back.

A couple of hours later, Mack and I were lounging side by side on the sofa watching TV. Rosie was on her phone as usual and Mum had her nose in a book.

I stretched and yawned. "I'll make us all a cuppa."

I'd just stood up when the front door banged and a moment later Derek rolled in, all merry after a few pints.

He saw me first and greeted me with a shoulder slap and a guy hug, ruffling my hair affectionately. He wasn't much of a hugger, Derek, but he got a bit more that way after a few beers.

When we broke apart, he spied Mack on the sofa, and for an instant, he froze. It was only for an instant, but it might as well have been an hour. We all noticed, and I suspected we all knew why he paused. Having hugged me—something he rarely did—should he try to hug Mack too?

Eventually, he seemed to make a decision and stepped toward Mack but Mack stayed where he was, his expression strained and almost panicky. Derek checked himself mid-stride, his hands curling into fists at his side, his cheeks flushing.

"Good to see you, Dylan," he said with awkward formality. "It's been a while."

"It's only been a week," Mack replied, his tone abrupt. And fair enough. Given how many years had passed without him seeing his Dad at all, a week wasn't worth mentioning.

There was an uncomfortable silence.

"So, Derek," I said, sitting myself down again. I'd decided a change of subject was in order. "I had the meeting with Fletchers' Delis today."

"Without me?" Derek turned to me, frowning.

"Mum said you couldn't make it because of Rosie's appointment."

His frown deepened and his voice was irritable when he replied. "Well, couldn't you have rearranged the meeting? You knew I wanted to go!"

I suspected he was redirecting his angry embarrassment over what had just happened with Mack at me, but frankly, I was so fucked off, I didn't care what the reason was. Since I'd started on my retail project, Derek had done nothing but bitch and complain, disagreeing with everything I suggested, yet insisting on being included, every step of the way. And if he'd really wanted to be at the meeting, why hadn't he *asked* me to rearrange it?

I opened my mouth to bite out a terse reply but before I could say anything, to my shock, Mack blurted out, "Nathan was amazing—he had them eating out of his hand. You should be thanking him, not criticising him."

Derek blinked at him. "You were there?"

"Yeah," Mack said flatly, offering no explanation.

Derek's gaze shifted between us.

"So, what did they say?" he asked at last, turning back to me. "Did you show them the packaging designs? What did they think?"

"I showed them all the designs," I said. "They liked the contemporary ones."

Derek's brows knotted. "What? But they're all wrong. Who wants to buy tiny little cartons of ice cream like that?"

I was usually pretty even-tempered, but that got to me. Derek was quite happy to leave the business to me when it came to running the café or doing the books. But this? *This* he wanted to be in charge of?

When marketing was what I *did*?

Biting back the desire to tell him to *fuck off*, I said calmly, "The point of the meeting was to get the benefit of the Fletchers' retail expertise. They sell luxury produce, day in day out. They know what their customers want and they said that—"

"Yes, but you can't just think about the one or two dozen people popping into the local deli!" Derek interrupted. "If we want to take this nationwide, we need to appeal to the masses."

I huffed out a frustrated sigh. "Derek, we're not bloody Walls! We can't compete with mass-market products. We want to aim for a smaller luxury market—"

"No, *you* want to aim for that. *I* don't." Derek snapped.

"Derek!" Mum said sharply.

"What?" he said, throwing his hands in the air. "This is *my* business, if you remember, Lorraine."

I opened my mouth to point out that it wasn't, not anymore, but before I could say a word, Mack beat me to it.

"Christ, you're ungrateful!" he exclaimed, his Scottish accent more pronounced than I'd ever heard it. He glared at his father, lip curling. "Nathan does everything around here. *Everything*. And it's obvious he started way before Rosie got ill. He sorts out the work rotas and makes sure all the shifts are covered. When he can't cover a shift, he does it *himself* on top of all his own shifts. He does all the paperwork. He gets all the supplies in. He banks all the takings and pays all the bills. And this retail thing was all *his idea*. Not yours. Not anyone else's. *His*." He gave a huff of disgust. "And you. What do you do? Spend a few hours a day on your own, making ice cream. That's it. That's your contribution. And you think that entitles you to make every decision?"

"I started this business up," Derek said hotly, jabbing himself in the chest with his thumb. "I think that entitles me to some say about what happens round here."

"Yeah, you're good at starting things off," Mack sneered. "Not got much appetite for putting in the hard graft over the long run though, are you?"

Derek went white. He looked at Mum, as though for support but her expression was uncharacteristically stony.

"Jonathan bailed us out," she said in a low, furious tone. "His inheritance stopped us losing the house. And *then* he gave up his job to come and help us sort out the mess. *Our* mess, Derek, not his!"

Derek swallowed. "I gave him half the shares in the company," he muttered, gaze shifting away.

"Exactly. He's an equal owner! And you know he was being generous only taking half the shares after what he sunk into the place. We were *this* close to liquidation!" She held her thumb and forefinger an inch apart, trembling with anger. "And Dylan's right about him doing the lion's share of the work. I *worry* about him, he does so much." She glanced at me then, her expression anxious. "I'm not much help either these days, and I'm so sorry, love."

My throat was tight with sudden emotion. I shook my head at her. "It's okay, Mum," I said hoarsely. "I know things have been hard lately."

"Lorraine's right," Derek said. I glanced at him but he was addressing Mack, his gaze bleak, his voice thick with self-loathing. "And so are you—about me dropping out when stuff gets tough. I dropped out of being a musician and a business owner, and worst of all, I dropped out of being a father. The truth is, I'm a fuck-up, Dylan. A failure. I don't even know why you—"

"No, Dad!" Rosie scrambled up from her chair and ran to him. "You're not a failure—you're not!" She burst into noisy tears, her arms tight round Derek's waist while he looked down at her, his expression pained.

"Rosie, I can't—oh, shit, don't cry, poppet, please . . ."

Mum went over to them, her angry expression morphing into one of pained concern as she put her arms round Rosie and met Derek's worried gaze over my sister's head.

I glanced at Mack, sitting next to me on the sofa. He looked sad and lost and strangely helpless. Like he didn't know what to do now.

"Do you want to leave?" I said in a low voice.

He nodded, his relief obvious.

"Come on then," I said, standing up.

"Jonathan, love, wait," Mum said. "Just for a minute. We should talk about—"

"Another time, Mum," I said, steering Mack to the door.

"But Derek needs to—"

"We can talk about it later," I said firmly. Her gaze shifted between me and Mack, and I thought I saw some kind of understanding in her eyes, but she didn't say anything, just nodded and let us go.

PROOF

CHAPTER SEVENTEEN

We walked back to the flat in silence. When we got in, I went straight to the kitchen and fetched a couple of beers. When I walked into the living room, Mack was just standing there, staring at the floor. He hadn't even taken off his beat-up leather jacket.

I set the beers down, tugged his jacket off his unresisting arms and steered him to the couch before handing him a bottle.

"Thanks," he muttered.

I sat beside him. "Are you okay?"

He sighed heavily. "Yeah, course." Lifted the bottle and took a deep drink. Stared into space.

"What's wrong?" It felt like a stupid question. I wasn't surprised he was upset, but I did wonder what in particular had him like this.

Eventually he looked at me. "You never told you me you were one of the owners of Dilly's."

I blinked at him. "Is that what's bothering you?"

"Why didn't you mention it? Why did you let me think my dad still owned it all?"

"Why does it matter?" I countered, frowning.

He leaned forward, elbows on his knees, dangling the beer bottle between his legs from loose fingers. All I could see was the back of his head, the defensive slope of his shoulders.

"I felt pretty stupid when I heard. I thought we—" He broke off, blew out some air. "Ah, fuck it. It doesn't matter."

My stomach sank. It did matter, whatever it was. I shifted, perching on the edge of the sofa so I could see him. In profile, he looked tired and I wanted to reach out to him. But I couldn't, because we didn't ever touch, not unless we were having sex. It was against the unspoken rules we'd somehow established.

"I'm sorry," I said. Made myself be honest. "I suppose I didn't mention it because I was uncomfortable about it. He's your dad and this started off as his business. Now I own half of it and . . ." I trailed off.

"And I don't own any of it?" He glared at me. "You think that would matter to me?"

"Not the money," I said. "But I thought it might, you know, hurt your feelings. Because of the family thing." I sighed. "I'm sorry. I should've told you."

His glare faded. "I see." He rubbed the back of his neck. "Okay, I get it. That makes sense. I should've realised it would be something like that. With it being you."

I burned to know what he meant by that, but didn't want to push too hard. He seemed to be in a fragile place and I was scared of tipping him over, so instead I just watched him, my stomach in knots.

"Nathan," he said after a while, still looking at his beer.

"Yeah?"

"Can we go to bed?"

I had to swallow against the lump in my throat to answer him. "Yeah."

He wanted me to fuck him.

He tried to make it into a fast, hard, anonymous quickie, just like he'd done that very first time. But just like that first time, I wasn't having it. I slowed everything down, made him lie on his back when he wanted to be on his hands and knees, kissed him all over, stretched and licked him till he was a puddle of throbbing want.

"God," he rasped at last. "Will you *please* fuck me, Nathan. I need you."

"I need you."

Those words.

I knew he only meant he needed me physically, but those words made my chest ache in the best way. I kissed him with every ounce of feeling that was in me, and when he kissed me back—not in that tongue-fucking way he'd got comfortable with, but tenderly—it felt like we must both, surely, be sharing that feeling.

I need you.

He was very ready for me when I finally sank my shaft inside him, his body drawing me in. I moaned into his mouth as he pulsed around me and he wrapped his long legs about my hips, tilting his pelvis to give me the best possible angle. I rocked into him with exploratory nudges, till he gave a gasping sob that told me I'd hit what I was looking for. And then I set about nudging that spot again, and again.

His body was wide open to me, his arms and legs holding me close, and even then, it wasn't enough. I didn't just want these naked moments of sexual pleasure and orgasm. I wanted more from him, an emotional connection. So I kept my mouth on his, kissing him, watching him, willing him to open his own eyes, which he finally did.

I love you.

I desperately wanted to say it. It was on the tip of my tongue, but I knew it would make him run. I just knew. So I stayed quiet. I was sure, though, that he must see in my eyes how I felt about him. Must taste it in every kiss I gave him. I might as well be wearing a sign that announced to the world that he was *it* for me, it was so painfully obvious.

I love you.

When it was over, when we'd both come hard, together, he drifted off in my arms. Asleep in my arms for the first time since the first night we met.

I remembered his words from that night.

"Hold me."

He hadn't had to ask this time.

When I woke up the next morning, I was alone.

I wasn't exactly surprised, but that didn't stop me feeling empty when I saw the space in the bed beside me.

I touched the pillow, still dented with the hollow that had cradled Mack's head as he slept, only to snatch my hand away again. Jesus, what was *wrong* with me? This wasn't me. I was pragmatic, resilient. I didn't moon over anyone; had never done that over any of my boyfriends.

The difference was, I was in love with Mack, and it was a deeper, sharper emotion than I'd ever experienced. Maybe I'd be happy if Mack felt the same way, instead of lying here, staring miserably at the ceiling.

Fuck it. Time to get up. I had the day off and had planned to stay in bed for a while, but I couldn't lie here any longer, brooding.

It was the first Saturday I'd been off in ages and I wondered what on earth I was going to do with myself. I'd got so used to spending what little free time I had with Mack, that I was at a loss. Maybe a run? It'd been a while since I'd done anything resembling exercise.

I dragged myself out of bed, pulled on my robe and wandered through the kitchen. I wasn't sure if I'd find Mack in there or not, but no, it was quiet. The living room was deserted too. Either he'd gone to his own bedroom and was still sleeping or he'd gone out.

I tried to banish from my mind the suspicion that he might've just packed up and left altogether. That was ridiculous. Even so, as I ate breakfast, staring unseeingly at some American sitcom repeat on TV, my attention was elsewhere, listening for sounds of Mack getting up or coming back to the flat.

Eventually, disgusted with myself, I put my running gear on and headed out.

I spent a good long time doing stretches before I headed off, making for Caerdu Castle. Once there, I'd loop round the coastal path to Mother Ivey's Bay and come back in at the other end of town. It was a decent six miles or so starting with a punishing climb so I'd be feeling it soon.

The day was wintry and cold. A mackerel sky stretched above me, a ripple of grey over steely blue. As I ran uphill towards the ruins of the castle, my thighs burned, lungs heaving far too soon. It was easier though, once I got to the headland. The gradient dropped to nothing and as I circled round on the coastal path, on the flat now, I began to enjoy myself at last.

The wind was strong up on the clifftops, ripping through my hair. Overhead, gulls screamed and kittywakes circled. It felt good to be outside. Why had I let my runs slide? It was crazy considering one of the reasons I'd agreed to come home had been to spend more time doing stuff like this.

I wished Mack was with me. I wanted to do all this stuff with him. All the ordinary, wonderful stuff that you found yourself desperate to share with a new lover. It hurt that I was never going to have that with him. Not the way I wanted anyway.

I ran past the life boat station and then I was on the home straight to Porthkennack, the wide, golden sweep of Mother Ivey's Bay to my left, at the bottom of the cliffs. The beach was almost empty of people at this time of year, though I spied a few dogwalkers and a family with a couple of little kids rockpooling. Another half mile took me off the uneven path and onto the flat tarmac road again. The buffeting wind and the cries of the gulls faded, replaced by the sounds of traffic and people.

I brought my pace down to a jog as I made my way through town back to the flat, gradually letting my muscles cool. By the time I reached my street, I'd slowed to a walk. Scrupulously, I performed my stretches then headed inside, feeling more centred and calm than I had in ages—until I strolled into the living room and saw that Mack was there. With Mum.

They sat on either end of the couch and Mum had clearly been crying. Her eyes were rimmed in black from where her mascara had run, and Mack was grim-faced. The atmosphere was strained.

"He feels terrible about everything," Mum was saying. "He just finds it difficult to tell you—he was trying to yesterday, before Rosie interrupted."

Mack said nothing.

She looked at me, her expression pleading. "Tell him, Jonathan."

"Tell him what?" I said flatly. I wasn't happy to find her here, doing Derek's dirty work—especially if she was trying to lay a guilt trip on Mack.

"That Derek's . . . well, he's *Derek*." She turned back to Mack. "He finds it hard to say sorry, even when he knows he's in the wrong, but that doesn't mean he isn't all torn up about this! You think he doesn't care but the truth is, he'll never forgive himself for leaving you." She shook her head. "He has so many hang-ups. You're probably not aware, but he had a difficult childhood—"

Mack physically recoiled at that, one hand going up, palm out.

"Lorraine, please stop. I don't want to hear it."

"But if you understood—"

"Mum," I snapped. "He said no!"

Her expression was wounded, and I added more gently, "You can't expect him to listen to this. Not if he doesn't want to."

She sighed, clearly defeated. "I know. I'm sorry." She looked back at Mack. "I know you feel he left you behind and I can only imagine how hard that was for you, but you deserve to know that it's not that he wasn't thinking about you all those years, and regretting his actions. Dylan, love, *no one* has regrets like your dad, but when anything comes up about emotions or feelings, he clams up. It's like he thinks if he lets himself feel . . ." She shook her head helplessly.

"Like he won't be able to push the feelings back inside," Mack finished for her. "Like maybe if he starts, he'll completely lose it."

Mum blinked at him, seeming surprised. "Yes," she said. "I think that's it."

I studied Mack, wondering what had prompted those words. If they described how he felt himself, or if that was how he saw his dad. Maybe it was both.

Mack sighed and rubbed a weary hand over the back of his neck. "I don't know what you want me to do here."

Mum said, "Just talk to him. Tell him how you feel."

He laughed. "Tell him how I *feel*? Christ, Lorraine, you don't ask much do you? I mean, Jesus, I already donated half my fucking liver to your kid! Now you want me cut my heart out and hand it to that old bastard on a plate? *No.* For fuck's sake!"

He got to his feet and paced away to the window. I wanted to help him but I wasn't sure there was anything I could do. So I stayed where I was, leaning against the wall, watching.

"You *do* feel something," Mum persisted.

He whirled around to face her, eyes blazing. "Feel something? Yeah, I feel something! I *feel* abandoned by him. I *feel* angry that the moment he met you lot he forgot all about me!" He swept his arm in my direction. "I *feel* resentful that he was more of a dad to Nathan than he ever was to me!"

I swallowed against a lump in my throat and looked away, guilt and misery churning in me. In that moment, I felt his resentment like a wave crashing down on me. *He must hate me. Hate all of us.*

"Nathan—" Mack's voice was hoarse, pleading, and when I glanced at him, his expression was raw and naked, every bit of his mask ripped away.

"I'm sorry," he said. "I don't resent *you.*"

"You should. I would."

His gaze was bleak. "It's not your fault. I know that."

"It's not yours either," I pointed out, because I had a feeling that, deep down, Mack thought that maybe it was. Or at least that Derek hadn't come back because Mack hadn't been worth the bother.

Mum stood up then. I'd almost forgotten she was there.

"I'm sorry I upset you, love," she told Mack, dabbing at her eyes with a tissue. "I'll give you some peace to think. Just please remember: the only reason I'm saying this at all is because I desperately want us all to be a family. I blame myself for allowing this to go on. Derek insisted it was best to let sleeping dogs lie, but I always knew that wasn't right. I should've insisted he fix things."

Mack didn't answer.

"I'll walk you out," I told Mum.

I went all the way downstairs with her to the main door that led out on to the street. As we stood there, on the front step, she looked me in the eye and said, "Something's going on between you two, isn't it?"

I didn't bother denying it. She knew me too well. "Yeah."

For a moment, she didn't say anything but her expression was concerned.

"What?" I asked.

"You're stepbrothers."

"So? It's not like we grew up together. We only met a few months ago." I didn't bother explaining that we'd met before I ever knew who he was.

"I know, but be prepared for people to gossip about it. This is a small town."

I gave a short laugh. "You needn't worry, I don't think this is going anywhere."

She looked relieved. "It's not serious then?"

"Not on his part."

My feelings about that must've shown because her face fell. "Oh, love," she said, eyes soft with sympathy. "Maybe he just can't tell you how he feels?"

I shook my head. "He's planning on heading off. Soon. Once he goes, I reckon it'll be the last any of us see of him." My voice broke a little on the last part and she reached for me, hugging me hard.

"Have you told him how *you* feel?" she whispered into my ear and I shook my head weakly.

She pushed back from me, hands on my upper arms, gaze searching mine. "You should tell him," she said. "I think he's more like his dad than he'd ever want to admit. He's aching to be loved, that boy. And you're so lucky—you got so much love growing up, from me and your dad and your nanny and grandad. And from Derek and Rosie. That gives you a core of strength, you know."

Chest aching, I admitted the painful truth. "I don't think he feels the same way."

"I don't believe that," she said fiercely. "But even if he doesn't, if you let him go without saying anything, you'll regret it one day. I know it's hard to face the possibility of rejection, and I know you find it hard to tell people what *you* want sometimes, love." She let me go but her gaze was still intent on mine. "But if you don't do that—don't speak up—you might find your chance is gone."

CHAPTER EIGHTEEN

When I got back up to the flat, Mack had his jacket on and his guitar case in hand.

"I'm going down to the pub," he said, avoiding my gaze. "I told Don I'd pop down today to chat through the playlist."

Tonight was Mack's debut—and maybe only—gig at the Sea Bell.

"It's only half-eleven." Did I sound desperate? More casually, I added, "Will they even be open yet?"

Mack shrugged. "Don asked me pop down before the lunchtime rush."

Yeah, I bet he did, I thought, remembering the guy's hand on Mack's bicep in the café and his ready smile.

Mack brushed past me on his way to the door and I considered, stopping him, asking him to wait a minute.

I need to tell you something.

In the end, though, I bottled it. If I was going to tell him how I felt, I needed to think about what I was going to say.

"I'll see you later then," I said instead.

"Yeah, later."

After he left, I stood there, in the middle of the living room, wondering if I'd made a mistake. If I should've grasped the nettle, right then. But it was too late for that now.

I showered and changed out of my running gear, made coffee, pottered round the flat. I was waiting for Mack to come back, turning over what I might say to him in my mind. Except he didn't come back.

It was nearly five when he texted me:

Eating dinner at pub. C u at gig later. M

Less than a minute later, my phone pinged again:

If ur coming that is. U don't have to. M

I read those texts about ten times before I finally texted him back:

Of course I'm coming. Idiot. N x

Once I'd sent it, I started fretting that he didn't actually want me there. A couple of minutes later, I got back:

Ok. I'm on at 9

Not so much as a smiley face to hint at his feelings. I stared at my phone, not sure what to think.

I walked down to the pub just after seven. The place was bustling with it being folk night, full to the brim with a mix of Jago's locals and the folk-music followers he tolerated for this one night each week. I greeted a few people I knew with smiles and waves but didn't stop to talk, heading straight for the bar.

I looked round for Mack while Jago poured my pint, eventually spotting him sitting at a table with a bunch of people—Don, of course, and two women, plus the ponytail guy—Andy?—we'd seen play here the night Mack arrived in Porthkennack. The five of them were surrounded by instruments—a few guitars, a banjo, a ukulele, a violin. I wondered if any of the others were playing tonight.

They were all smiling and laughing—Mack too, for once. He seemed comfortable. Unguarded in a way I'd not seen much before. I watched him over the lip of my pint, trying to put my finger on what it was about him that made him appear so at ease. For the first time I could remember, he looked like he felt *at home*. It was good seeing him like that, but it made my chest tight too.

I thought about going over there, to join him, but I worried that maybe I'd be intruding—it seemed unfair to barge in when he was so happy. I'd not seen him smiling this much in all the time I'd known him, and honestly, that made me sad. So, I turned back to the bar and gave my attention to my pint instead.

I'd almost finished my beer when I felt a light touch at my elbow. I lifted my head, and there he was, standing beside me.

His expression was . . . quizzical.

"When did you come in?" he asked gesturing at my almost empty glass.

I cleared my throat. "A while ago."

He frowned. "Didn't you see me?"

"I did, yeah."

His frown deepened. "Why didn't you come over then?"

I offered a half-smile. "You seemed busy."

For the longest moment he didn't say anything, then, so quietly I almost couldn't make it out, he said. "I'm never too busy for you, Nathan."

An unfamiliar emotion speared me. It was a bit like happiness and a bit like longing without being either one of those things.

"*I'm never too busy for you. . .*"

What did he mean by that? Did he have deeper feelings for me than I thought? I wanted to believe he did, but I suspected he only meant that he liked me as a friend, or worse, that he was grateful to me. And yet, I couldn't help but hope it meant more.

"You're not?" I said, meeting his steady, melting gaze, willing him to go on. But he didn't elaborate on what he meant, just shook his head and grinned.

"Course not. For God's sake, I've been hoping you'd arrive since I texted you."

The quick stab of joy I felt at hearing he'd wanted me, had been waiting for me, made me smile helplessly. I knew that the irrepressible hitch of my mouth must betray me and the part of me that was scared of my feelings, terrified at the prospect of Mack rejecting me, urged caution.

I tried to pack that smile away, saying as casually as I could manage, "I can't wait to see you play."

Yes, talk about music. That was a safe topic.

But when Mack glanced at me, he undid all my carefulness with just one teasing smile. "Yeah? You like to see me play?"

And that was it. My own betraying smile was back.

"Yeah, I do," I admitted, bumping his shoulder with mine.

Scintillating stuff, I know, but though our words were brief, it felt like something big was being said. Me, admitting how much I'd wanted to come here and him, admitting he'd wanted me here.

As small as these confessions were, right then, they seemed huge. The tiny, hopeful part of me began to wonder if Mum was right, if Mack might be ready to hear how I felt. Maybe even admit that he had feelings for me too? It was a dizzying thought.

We grinned at each other like idiots for a moment, then Mack said, "You want another beer?"

"Yeah, okay. I'll have another pint of Chough's Nest."

He made a face. "God, that stuff again?"

I laughed. "It's an acquired taste."

We stood companionably, side by side, as Jago pulled out our pints, our arms brushing. It was pretty low key as PDAs went, but it felt good, being able to casually, innocently touch him. I'd grown used to his impenetrable walls and finally, tonight, they were crumbling, just a little.

Jago set my reddish-brown pint down in front of me with a grunt before turning away to pour the generic lager Mack had selected.

"I can't believe you drink that," Mack said, eyeing my pint.

"At least my beer doesn't taste like watered-down piss."

He laughed, easy, dark eyes sparkling with humour and affection and my heart clenched.

Christ, I was a goner.

Once we had our drinks, Mack took me back to the table. We sat down and he and introduced me to the others: Don, Andy, Tash and Amy.

"Is this your other 'alf then?" Tash asked Mack as I shook her heavily ringed hand.

Before either of us could speak, Andy laughed. "Christ, no, Tash, they're *brothers*!"

Horrified, I said, "No—no, we're not."

Andy frowned in puzzlement. To Mack he said. "I thought you were both Dex's lads?"

"*I* am." Mack jerked his thumb at me, "But he's not. His mum married my dad"

"Oh right. You're *step*brothers," Don said, looking way too pleased.

I opened my mouth to explain just how recently we'd met, but Mack got in first, saying mildly, "Yeah, but we're also fucking each others' brains out."

It was such an uncharacteristically brash thing for him to say, I couldn't stop the burst of laughter that exploded out of me. And then everyone else laughed too. I'm not sure whether they believed him, but there were no more questions because right then Jago arrived at the table.

"Are none of you lazy bastards goin' to play tonight? It's bleddy eight o'clock!"

"Keep your 'air on," Tash said, rolling her eyes. But even as she said it, she was getting to her feet, as were Don and Amy. It turned out the three of them played together as the Shanteurs and they were up before Mack. They decamped to a tiny stage area that had been cordoned off by the windows, prompting a few whoops at this sign that folk music night was about to get going. The crowd began to shift so that most everyone was facing the stage.

The reason for the name of the group was obvious once they started playing—they had a sort of sea shanty vibe going on and Mack watched them play with rapt attention, glancing at me occasionally to smile, sharing his pleasure in the music. They were accomplished musicians and Amy had a sweet, pure voice that the crowd loved. I wondered if it made Mack more nervous about his own set, seeing them get such a good reception, but if it did, he didn't show it.

When it was his turn, he strolled up to the tiny stage area, sharing a few laughs with the others as they packed up their instruments and removed the extra stools. Then he settled his guitar strap over his neck, perched himself on the single high stool, they'd left for him, and without a word, began to play.

He started with my favourite, *Carrickfergus*, not so much launching as sliding into it, with a long instrumental opening that slowly quieted the chattering crowd till they were entirely silent. Till he held them in the palm of his hand.

When he eventually began to sing, it seemed to me that he sounded different than all the other times I'd heard him. His voice was as deep and rich as ever but tonight there was a regretful, melancholy note in it that brought a salty lump to my throat. Or maybe it was the words of the song, because—God, how had I never heard it before?—this song was about *Mack*. The song of a man who insisted he was happy with his life roving from town to town, but who longed for some vision of home he could never quite find.

And all I could think was, *I want to be his home.*

"Mack, wait!"

We were on our way out the pub when Don called to Mack from the bar and started squirming his way through the close-packed bodies towards us.

"We were just heading off," Mack told him when he finally reached us.

Don grinned. "I wanted to catch you before you went. Listen, do you want to play again next Saturday? You could have the same slot if you like."

I felt Mack's discomfort at the question and knew why he hesitated. His threemonth scan was on Thursday—by next Saturday he might be on his way back to Manchester, or Scotland . . .or Spain. I tried to look like I wasn't really listening, but in truth I was as interested in the answer to Don's question as Don himself.

Mack frowned. "Um . . . can I get back to you?"

My heart sank and Don's grin faded a bit too. "Okay, sure. But can you let me know in the next couple of days? It's the first weekend in December next week so nights out are starting to happen and it gets more difficult to book people."

"Yeah, yeah, I'll do that," Mack promised.

"Great. Text me to let me know. See you soon." Don clapped Mack on the shoulder and strolled away.

We emerged from the pub into a night that was cold and clear, the dark, velvet firmament above us dotted with pin-bright stars. I zipped the last couple of inches of my jacket up to my chin and burrowed my hands deeper into my pockets.

"You were amazing tonight," I said.

Mack smiled at me, but his eyes were sad. "Thanks."

We fell silent as we began walking, but after a bit I said, trying to keep my voice light, "Why didn't you say yes to that gig? Don't you want to play at the Sea Bell again?" I didn't look at Mack as I waited for his answer, staring straight ahead instead. The sea front was at the bottom of the hill, black waves glinting in the moonlight.

He didn't respond immediately, but at last he said, "Yeah. I want to. It was great."

"Why not just agree then?"

He sighed, heavily. "You know why, Nathan."

I stopped walking, coming to a halt right in the middle of the street. He took a couple of steps past me before he realised, then he stopped too, turning to glance back at me warily.

"Tell me anyway," I said.

He met my gaze and his own was unwavering. "I've got my scan next week," he said. "I'm pretty sure I'll get discharged—I feel completely normal. And after that? Well, it's about time I got going."

"Bullshit." My voice was harsh. Angry.

For a moment he appeared oddly pained, but then he got his expression under control and said quietly, "I never intended to stay, Nathan. You knew that."

I thought about Mum's words that morning.

Those moments at the bar—"*I'm never too busy for you.*"

The sense I'd had as he sang that his determined insistence he wanted to move on wasn't necessarily true.

I stepped towards him, taking hold of his upper arms.

"You don't have to go. And I don't want you to. I want you to stay, Mack."

He stared at me, his face suddenly stricken.

"I'm *asking* you to stay. Please, Mack. Give us a chance." My voice cracked on the words, betraying me, betraying how true those words were, and how hopeless they felt. How afraid I was.

But Mack just . . . shook his head.

He shook his fucking head.

"Listen, Nathan, I don't want—" He broke off and swallowed hard, throat bobbing.

I dropped my hands from his arms and stepped back, angry pride coming to my rescue. "What?" I demanded. "Tell me."

I stood there, looking him in the eye, giving him every chance to tell me what was going through his head. But he only stared at me, his throat working, unable, apparently, to articulate his thoughts.

At last, I realised he wasn't going to say anything, and that hurt like a motherfucker.

"Okay," I said, as my heart shattered into a million pieces. "Okay."

I turned and began to walk away. And he didn't even try to stop me.

CHAPTER NINETEEN

The next morning, I called Denise and asked if she'd cover my shift at the cafe. It was obvious things were going to be uncomfortable between me and Mack and I wanted to make sure we spoke as early as possible. Re-established some kind of normality. I showered and dressed and sat myself down in the living room with my laptop to wait him out.

It was close to lunchtime when he finally appeared, his expression wary. I greeted him as though nothing had happened, poured him a coffee from the pot I'd just made and launched into a monologue of inane small talk. He looked a bit shell-shocked at first, but eventually he rallied and it did the job of breaking the worst of the ice. More importantly, it made it clear that I had no intention of revisiting the embarrassing subject I'd raised the night before.

Presumably he was grateful for that.

After that, things went back to a sort of normal. We were civil with each other, but we didn't talk the way we had before. I went out in the evenings, round to Mum's or up to the Bell for a pint. By the time I'd get back, Mack would be in bed. Sometimes I heard him playing his guitar in there, which he hadn't done before.

Our interactions were few and, for me, painful. I adopted a kind of distantly friendly persona that felt awkward as hell and Mack just went very quiet. Occasionally I'd catch him looking at me with a melancholy expression that made me more angry than anything else, though I pretended not to notice it.

I thought a lot about those humiliating few moments, when I'd begged him to stay and he'd turned me down. He hadn't said much but one thing was clear: he didn't return my feelings. Well, fine. I was a big boy. I'd live. I had too much to do to sit around being heartbroken. I had a business to run, plans to make and a ton of people relying on me to keep everything together.

Work kept me going. Work, work and more work.

On the Wednesday night, Mack cornered me in the kitchen.

"Can I have a word?"

"Sure." I'd just stacked the dishwasher and I busied myself wiping down the counters so I didn't have to meet his gaze. "What's up."

"I've got my scan tomorrow."

I glanced up at that. "Yeah, I know. I was going to ask if you want a lift up to the hospital."

He shook his head. "I'll get the bus. It's not till eleven so I've got ages to get there."

I hesitated. "You don't, you know, want someone to go with you?"

He looked away. "No, it's fine."

Of course. Mack didn't need anyone, least of all me.

"The thing is," he went on. "I said to Don I'd play that gig at the Sea Bell on Saturday so I was wondering if it'd be okay if I stayed till then? I know it's a couple of days more than you probably thought . . ." He trailed off and met my gaze, his own wary.

He thought I wanted him gone as soon as possible. Maybe that was a reasonable assumption but the truth was, I felt sick at the thought of him going. Despite everything, I still didn't want him to leave, and how pathetic was that? Hot prickles at the back of my eyes warned me how close I was to humiliating myself again. I turned away to the sink, running hot water over a cloth and wringing it out. Busy work.

"Yeah, no problem," I said lightly. "I said at the start you could stay as long as you needed. Nothing's changed."

I began methodically wiping down the sink, swallowing hard against the stubborn lump in my throat. For what felt like ages, Mack was silent. Eventually he said. "Thanks. I really appreciate it. I'll be out of your hair by Monday."

Moments later, the kitchen door closed behind him.

I stood there at the sink, looking out the window at the cobbled, rain-slick streets of my home town. It was a cold December day in Porthkennack, gloomy and grey, and it kind of felt like that in my heart too.

"I'll be out of your hair by Monday."

Mack's scan was fine. I was at Mum's when he popped round to tell her. His liver was growing back well, he explained, over the cup of tea Mum had pressed on him. The specialist was happy with his progress and he'd been formally discharged.

"So that's it?" Mum said, frowning. "You won't be seen again?"

Mack shook his head. "Not here. They said I'll need an annual check-up but I can do that through my own doctor." He smiled at her. "The point is, I'm fine. Everything's good."

Mum didn't look happy, and honestly, I wasn't either. Would Mack follow up with his own doctor? He'd be stupid not to—and he wasn't a stupid guy—but right now he didn't even know where he was going to be living. I could see him putting a check-up off if he wasn't settled somewhere when he needed it.

"What's good?" That was Rosie. She stood in the kitchen doorway in her school uniform. She'd put on weight, lost the sallow cast to her skin and the shadows under her eyes. She'd have to keep taking the immuno-suppressants but other than that, she was not just better, she was cured. Mack's liver had replaced her own diseased organ with a new healthy one that her body had accepted. And with her condition now under control with medication, there was no reason her new liver should suffer any future damage.

He'd saved her life.

"*I'm* good," Mack said, smiling at her. "I had my scan today—everything's fine. I've been discharged."

She grinned. "That's great!"

"I still think it's a bit soon to be discharging you," Mum said, worriedly.

"Stop fussing, Mum." Rosie rolled her eyes at Mack. He grinned back at her and for a second I saw a flash of resemblance between them. They didn't look that much alike, but there were moments sometimes, when their facial expressions aligned, when, I saw it.

Rosie was going to miss him terribly. Had he even told her he was leaving?

"So, can I come to your gig on Saturday?" she asked, plonking herself down at the kitchen table and grabbing a Hobnob. "I really want to see you play."

"I don't think they let under-eighteens in after nine at the Bell," Mack said.

Rosie scowled and turned to Mum. "Can't you have a word with Jago?"

"I could try," Mum said, though her tone was doubtful. She glanced at Mack. "It would be a shame for her to miss out on your last gig."

"What?" Rosie had been reaching for another Hobnob but now she let her arm drop to the table, her gaze on Mack disbelieving. "Are you *leaving*?"

So he hadn't told her.

"I never intended to stay long-term," Mack said gently. "You know that, Ro."

"But—but I thought you'd changed your mind? You're working at the café and giving me guitar lessons and playing gigs at the Bell. It's been *great*. Why do you want to leave?"

"It's not that simple."

"Yeah, it is," she replied angrily. "What else have you got going on anyway? It's not like you've got some fantastic job lined up somewhere else, is it? Or a secret boyfriend stashed away?"

Mack's cheeks flushed. Mine probably did too, but she wasn't looking at me, thankfully.

"Rosie!" Mum snapped. "Stop it!"

Rosie ignored her. "And what about Dad?"

Mack's jaw ticked. "What about him?" he said tightly.

"Things need to get fixed between you."

He didn't pretend not to know what she was talking about. "Some things can't be fixed. That's how it is between me and Dad."

"No," she said, and it was a demand and a plea at once. "If Dad could say sorry, really apologise properly, this *could* be fixed."

"Rosie!" Mum snapped.

Rosie glared at her. "What? Someone's got to say something! Or are we all just going to pretend this isn't weird and wrong?"

I glanced at Mack. His expression was hard but I could see from the bleakness in his gaze that he was distressed. Flatly he said, "My relationship with Dad's none of your business."

"Of course it is," Rosie replied angrily. "You're my brother and he's my dad and the whole thing's so screwed up it's ridiculous. I *know* Dad's sorry, I *know* he loves you!"

Mack stood up so suddenly, his chair screeched against the floor tiles. "You have no idea!" he hissed. "When I was your age, my mum *died* and you know what Dad did when I told him to fuck off? Just once? *He did it*! He fucked off and he never came back." Mack raked a hand through his hair. Said more quietly, "You have literally no idea how that feels."

"Dylan, love—" Mum started, but Rosie spoke over her.

"You want to talk about what happened to *me* at fifteen?" she asked, jerking a thumb at her chest. "A doctor sat me down and told me that if I didn't get a liver transplant, I was going to die."

I sucked in a breath. "Jesus, Rosie, it's not a competition!"

She met my gaze and her eyes were blazing. "I don't mean it like that! I mean that something's happened to me that hasn't happened to any of you. When you think you're going to die, a lot of stuff looks different. You see how temporary you are. You see you're not going to get second chances at things." She turned back to Mack. "If you go now, there might never be another chance to fix this. And I know it's hurting you. You *and* Dad."

Honestly, I was stunned. I'd assumed she was oblivious to those undercurrents.

Not so, apparently.

I glanced at Mack and he seemed so lost, so fucking *alone*. I wished I could comfort him. Instead I had to sit there, clenching my fists under the table, watching helplessly as he considered Rosie's words.

"Just talk to him, Dylan," Rosie begged. "Please."

"Why should I?" he said bleakly. "He's the one who fucked up."

Rosie said, "I know, I'm not asking you to make the first move, only, not to leave yet. To give him a chance to sort this out." She paused, then added, "I wouldn't ask if I wasn't sure you need this as much as he does. But I think you do, Dylan. I think this makes you really sad."

Honestly, I didn't know if I agreed with Rosie or not, but it was impossible to ignore her sheer force of belief. Was she right? Did Mack need to mend things with Derek, if only for his own peace of mind? He'd gone all these years without his dad, and it wasn't as if over these last few months they'd grown any closer. Did he need Derek in his life at all? Was he just better off without him?

I watched Mack, trying to read him. He huffed out a long breath and scrubbed his hands over his face. When he finally looked up again, his expression was anguished.

"I don't know," he said at last. "I wouldn't even know how to start the conversation. I'm no good with words." He glanced at me, then away quickly, as though he hadn't intended to do it, and my heart ached for him.

"Well," Mum said slowly. "it doesn't have to be a big, heavy thing. You don't have to launch straight into talking about the past. Just arrange to spend a little time with him. Find some common ground. You're both musicians after all—it shouldn't be that hard."

"Invite him to your gig on Saturday!" Rosie said excitedly. "Take Nathan—you can call it a—a boys' night out."

"What about me?" Mum said, indignantly. "I was planning on going."

"You talk too much," Rosie said, leaning down to kiss her on the cheek. "They'll never end up speaking to each other if you go."

I couldn't help chuckling at Mum's offended expression. "Oi," she said. "I'm not that bad."

Rosie looked at Mack. "Will you do it?"

"I don't know," Mack said but I could tell the fight had gone out of him. He was going to agree. And Rosie's smile told me she knew it too.

CHAPTER TWENTY

Chorus
I'll be hanging up my Christmas stocking
So, when Santa comes a-knocking
There will be a place for him
To put my Christmas presents in
But I don't need no fancy parcels
I don't want no bows or sparkles
All I want this Christmas Day
Is you telling me that you are gonna stay.
Christmas Stocking by The Sandy Coves, 1989

December

Derek's arrival at the Sea Bell on Saturday night was greeted with a barrage of friendly insults from the locals.

"What you doing 'ere?" Jago asked when we reached the bar. "You usually drink in the Eagle."

"I've come to see my lad play, haven't I?" Derek replied, jerking his head at the table where Mack—who'd come earlier—was already sitting with Don and the others, his usual pissy lager sitting in front of him.

Jago nodded at that. "Chip off the old block that one, I reckon."

Derek visibly brightened. "Yeah?" He glanced at Mack again, plainly curious.

"Had me nearly bawling my eyes out last time he played," Jago said, stretching for a glass for Derek's whisky. A man of few words,

Jago, and not many of them compliments, so this was high praise indeed. I glanced at Derek. He was doing that thing he sometimes did where he projected an air of confident *bonhomie* but was secretly a bit anxious. I could tell from the way he bounced on his heels and kept looking around; from the way his smile kept fading and having to be topped up. I even felt weirdly protective to him for a moment, which was ridiculous, not to mention misplaced—of the two of them, it was Mack I was more concerned about tonight—yet I couldn't help but react to Derek's obvious nervousness.

Fixer, you see.

It was funny, really. My own parents were pretty similar types—both solid and dependable—but, for whatever reason, their marriage hadn't lasted. Derek was a bloody mess, but he was the sun, moon and stars as far as Mum was concerned. I still remembered the mortifying vows they'd made at their wedding when I was a spotty teenager. Mum going on about Derek being the love of her life. I'd wanted to retch at the time, but it was true. Maybe the reason they'd lasted was because he needed her so much and she had such a lot to give. Both of Derek's previous marriages had failed because of cheating, but in all the years he'd been with Mum, I'd never so much as seen him glance at another woman, so who knew what he'd been searching for till then.

Relationships were weird. *People* were weird.

I glanced over at the table where Mack sat and my heart clenched. He seemed nervous too, but there was no *bonhomie* on his part. He might have been going to his own execution. I wished I could just wave a magic wand and make things right between him and Derek. Or at least, right enough that their relationship didn't feel completely broken.

Once we had our drinks, I led Derek over to Mack's table. Andy was there and Derek greeted him by name so plainly knew him, at least a little. Mack introduced him to Don and another guy, dark-haired with a greying beard, called Ben who told Derek he was "*a big fan*". No sign of Tash or Amy tonight.

Everyone shifted round so we could all sit in the booth. Somehow I ended up between Mack and Derek which felt all wrong, not to mention being some kind of awkward metaphor. I made a mental note to nip off to the gents in five minutes so they'd have to sit together.

"Hey, you're Dex MacKenzie!" Ben said after a minute. "I'd heard you lived round here."

That pleased Derek. He smiled wide. "Yeah, I run the ice cream place near the Tesco Express."

I had to suppress the urge to roll my eyes at that one—it'd been years since Derek had *run* anything. I glanced at Mack who offered an understanding quirk of a smile.

And then Ben started on about—of all bloody things—Derek's failed solo album.

"That was a great album, man. Some of songs on there—what was that one, *Just Like Me*? Gorgeous. What was going on with your record company? They didn't promote it at all."

Right then, Derek looked strangely vulnerable. I'd heard him ranting a few times over the years about his treatment at the hands of his record company, but here, now, faced with someone honestly praising his music, he didn't seem pissed off at all. Just sort of grateful, and maybe sad.

"That's a good song," Mack agreed. "*Just Like Me*, I mean."

Derek stared at him, surprised. "You like it?" he said at last.

Mack cleared his throat. "Yeah, that little instrumental opening—that's lovely."

"And that first line," Ben interjected. "God, what a gut punch. The words on that song, man."

Mack nodded agreement and Derek's throat bobbed with emotion.

I tried to remember the song they were talking about but I couldn't. Derek occasionally played that album when he was a bit drunk and nostalgic, but I can't say I'd paid it much attention.

I excused myself and went to the gents. When I came back, I slipped into the other side of the booth next to Don, leaving Mack and Derek sitting together. Then I just leaned back and listened. It was all music talk, so I didn't have anything to add, but I was happy letting the others talk. After a while, I offered to get another round in, and when I got back from the bar, they were on to guitars, first guitars specifically, Derek talking about saving up some of the money he earned as a milk boy for his first Fender.

Mack seemed surprised by this. "I never knew you were a milk boy."

"Yeah," Derek said. "I used to get up at five every morning—well, six days a week. Could hardly keep my eyes open in school." He laughed, but Mack frowned.

"How old were you?"

"Twelve when I started—my mam needed the money. My dad had left and there were five of us. I gave her most of my wages but I got to keep a bit for myself and there were tips sometimes." He shrugged, then winked at Andy. "That's my excuse for doing so shite at school."

Funny, Derek talked about himself a lot, but not about his childhood. Not about his days as a milk boy. It was always the glory days he spoke about: touring with the band, going on Top of the Pops, having a single at number two in the charts.

I glanced at Mack. He appeared thoughtful, unaware of my scrutiny as he watched Derek banter with Andy and Ben.

When it came time for Mack's set, he got ready with his usual laid-back ease.

"He doesn't seem nervous, does he?" Derek murmured to me.

"No," I agreed. "He always looks really relaxed."

"He's like his mother," Derek said. "I used to get terrible nerves whenever I played but Tammy was always laid-back." He watched as Mack plugged in cables then tuned his guitar. "He's like her in a lot of ways."

"Yeah?" I said, trying not to seem too interested. "What ways?"

"I was always about 'making it' but Tammy wasn't ambitious—She just loved to play and sing."

I smiled. "That sounds like Mack."

"Why do you call him that?" Derek asked, and mortifyingly, I felt myself flush.

"I don't know," I mumbled. "He mentioned it was a nickname his friends used—I probably called him it a couple times and the habit stuck."

Derek opened his mouth to say more, but I was saved from whatever it was by Mack starting to play. From that moment on, I don't think I could have got Derek's attention if I'd fired a pistol next to his ear.

I watched him on-and-off as Mack played his set. He was strange sometimes, my stepdad. He acted so macho, but if something touched him, he'd get all watery-eyed and emotional. I found it a bit odd. My own dad found macho posturing ridiculous, but in a way he was tougher. You'd never catch him with tears in his eyes over a song, like Derek was, when Mack played *Carrickfergus*.

I caught Jago out the corner of my eye sniffing at that one too.

Towards the end of his set, Mack got a strange, thoughtful expression on his face. He'd just finished a song, but instead of launching into the next one straight away, he played a few experimental chords, mouthed a few words to himself. Then he pulled the microphone close.

"I know it's a bit early days for Christmas songs, but would you like to hear one?" he asked the crowd.

There were a few whoops of encouragement and Jago shouted, "It's December, lad, it's open season now!" Laughter at that.

Mack grinned. "All right." He strummed a couple of chords, then stopped and leaned forward again. "I love this song. It's beautiful." He played a few more chords and I noticed Derek stiffen in his seat.

"You'll know it," Mack assured the crowd. "But you'll be familiar with my dad's version. This is my version."

A few curious faces turned towards our table as Mack began picking out the introductory bars of a tune that was familiar to me but that I couldn't quite place yet. Derek clearly knew it though, since he was staring at Mack in astonishment.

And then Mack began to sing.

"Do you remember last December?
We were so in love last year..."

It was Derek's big Christmas hit, *Christmas Stocking*, but not like I'd ever heard it before. The version I knew had an obnoxious beat, catchy tune and silly video. This was entirely different. It was slow and sweet and sad. It was like Mack had found the real, authentic version of the song and polished it up like an uncut gem.

"I don't need no fancy parcels
I don't want no bows or sparkles..."

I'd never even noticed how much longing was in that song, the meaning of the words masked by synthesisers and electronic sleighbells. Sometimes we watched the old Christmas Top of the

163

Pops episode when the band had performed—or rather mimed—the song on TV like they were at some demented office party, grinning like maniacs with strands of tinsel round their necks and Christmas jumpers on.

I'd never really listened to it before, but now, in Mack's hands, it was a different song. A sad song.

A song about being left behind.

And yeah. Derek's eyes were wet.

We walked home from the pub, leaving Derek at the end of Eldertree Avenue. Mack's goodbye to his dad was muted but, for once, friendly. It felt like . . . well, an improvement anyway. The start of something, maybe, that might end up with a proper conversation. One day.

Derek got twenty yards down the street then he stopped and yelled, "Dylan!"

We turned back.

"You were great tonight, son!"

Dylan lifted an arm in acknowledgement. Father and son looked at each other for a long moment, then Derek turned and started trudging home.

Mack and I walked back to the flat, side by side, both of us quiet. It was a cold night and we both had our hands stuffed in our pockets, shoulders hunched. My breath plumed white on the freezing air and the cobbles under our feet were a little slippy with incipient frost.

I debated whether to say something about the evening, or just let it lie. In the end, I figured an observation couldn't hurt.

"That was generous of you," I said quietly. "Singing Derek's song, and saying those nice things about it. I could tell it meant a lot to him."

Mack glanced at me. His expression was uncertain. "Do you think?" he said. "I'm not good at stuff like that. Been too long on my own, probably. I'm rubbish at telling people how I feel."

I smiled at him, probably a sad sort of smile, if how I felt was anything to go by. "You're not the only one. It's not easy to open your heart."

Mack stopped walking.

"Nathan," he said hoarsely. "About what you said. Last week—"

Oh fuck, no. Not now.

"It's fine, Mack" I said quickly. "I shouldn't have said—"

"No, listen, I—"

I turned to him. "*Please* don't."

"But—Jesus, Nathan, please listen, I'm *so* sorry that I hurt you."

Humiliation tore at me. "It's fine, honestly. Can we not do this?"

"But what if—what if I've changed my mind? Maybe it's time I gave something like this—*us*—a try."

What. The. Fuck?

I stared at him, unable to parse what he was saying to me. What *was* he saying? That he was prepared to give me some kind of trial run? Test drive a relationship with me like I was a solid but not very exciting Ford Mondeo?

The surge of anger that overtook me at that thought surprised me.

I was fed up being everyone's rock—dependable old Nathan.

I was fed up coming at the end of every queue.

I was fed up being taken for granted.

I felt so hurt that I couldn't even speak. I shook my head.

Mack looked suddenly worried. He stepped toward me, reaching out a hand to me. "Nathan? Did I say something wrong?"

"I think I better take a walk," I said, whirling round and setting off.

"Wait," Mack said, hurrying after me. "I'll come with you."

I paused my step, glanced over my shoulder. "I need to be alone right now."

He froze, dark gaze wounded.

"Okay," he breathed, "If that's what you want."

"It is," I said shortly. And in that moment, I meant it.

PROOF

CHAPTER TWENTY-ONE

I stalked down to the sea-front and made my way onto the beach. Ignoring the biting wind, I settled down on the cold sand, huddling into my jacket as I stared at the black waves, letting the soothing rush and whisper of their ebb and flow wash over me. When I'd left home for university, I'd missed that sound more than anything.

I sat there for a long while, trying to get my head round what had happened with Mack. It was like I was trapped in a weird sort of dissonance that wouldn't let me sort through my thoughts—I just kept remembering his words and then I'd feel sick with resentment and a sharp sadness that hurt in a gut-deep way.

Distantly, I was aware that I was wallowing in self-pity, but couldn't seem to shake the feeling off. The thought kept returning to me that I'd been letting myself be put last by everyone for a long time, and the fact that I suspected I may have had a hand in causing that to happen myself didn't make me feel any better. I had a bad habit of encouraging other people not to worry about me, even as I tried to sort out their problems. But honestly, didn't it ever occur to anyone else that I might sometimes need help?

But you always insist you don't . . . an insidious voice at the back of my mind murmured.

I did do that, I knew. It was a habit I'd picked up my mother's knee, though whether I'd got it from copying her actions or whether it was written into the genes, I didn't know.

What I did know was that I'd been pushing myself too hard for too long. I felt so fucking tired of everything suddenly, like I had nothing left to give. Like I was all used up—no good to anyone.

I wanted someone to take care of *me* for a change.

And then, I remembered that day when Mack had gone off at Derek. Ice-cream-gate. It was pathetic how much it'd meant to me to have him stick up for me like that—not just because he did it, but because he did it without me having to ask. Because he'd noticed how much I was doing and he'd minded on my behalf.

Was that my problem? That I wanted to not have to ask for things? That I wanted people to be thinking about me so much that they not only anticipated my needs, they actually read my mind and knew when I was bullshitting about being fine?

That sounded pretty fucking self-absorbed. but yeah, maybe I did want someone to do that.

Like with ice-cream-gate.

Or like the day Mack offered to come to meet the Fletchers with me.

Or like the time he told me Mum and Derek asked too much of me.

Like all the times he'd pushed me back down onto the couch and insisted on making dinner or fetching me a cup of tea instead of the other way round.

Yeah, so maybe Mack was actually quite good at thinking about me . . .

But was that enough? What was it he'd said to me tonight? *"Maybe it's time I gave something like this—us—a try."*

It wasn't exactly the love declaration of the year—pretty far from the stuff that dreams were made of—but then I *knew* Mack found it difficult to say what he felt, ask for what he wanted. He'd told me as much.

And anyway, who was I to judge him for that? Jesus, I might be even worse at asking for things than he was. So why had I felt so angry? Why had his words upset me so much?

I knew the answer, of course, but it was hard to face up to the fact that Mack may not feel quite the same way that I did. That while I was in love with him, he only liked me enough to give being together a try. I already knew from the relationships I'd had before that if that was how Mack felt, he wasn't going to magically fall spectacularly in love with me later. If our feelings were unequal now, they were probably going to stay that way.

And I didn't want that.

I didn't want to be in another relationship like the ones I'd been in half a dozen times before—only this time with the roles reversed. I didn't want to be his Ford Mondeo—I wanted to be his gleaming two-seater sports car. Not that Mack was the sort of guy who would ever want a sports car, but whatever the equivalent of that was for him. Maybe the best guitar ever made.

I wanted to be his favourite. His best. I wanted him to feel for me what I felt for him. But the fact was, he didn't.

By now, the cold had penetrated through the layers of my clothing and I began to shiver.

Slowly, stiffly, I rose, and headed for home.

Mack was still up.

When I walked into the living room, he got off the sofa and stepped towards me, then stopped in his tracks.

"You're back," he said, somewhat redundantly.

"Yeah."

"I was getting worried— You were ages and it was so cold tonight . . ."

"Yeah, sorry. I needed to think for a bit." I pulled off my knit hat and unzipped my jacket.

His eyes, dark and anxious, moved over my face, trying to read me. "I was thinking about what I said," he began, "I wondered if maybe you'd thought again and realised you didn't really want to give things a go with me after all . . ." He trailed off.

I met his gaze. It was tempting to take that face-saving way out, but it would be a lie, and I couldn't tell him a barefaced lie, even if it did shred my pride to admit the truth.

"It wasn't that."

"Then I don't understand"—he swallowed hard and rubbed the back of his neck—"Why were you so angry? I thought you might actually be *pleased*, you know?" This was hard for him, I could see that. The least he deserved was an honest answer.

I braced myself. "I don't want you to start something with me because of *my* feelings."

His frown deepened. "What?"

"The only reason you should stay with someone is because *you* want to."

He blinked, seeming none the wiser.

Abandoning the last remnants of my pride, I muttered, "I don't want to be with someone who doesn't love me back."

For a long, awful moment he said nothing. Heat crept up my neck and into my face in a slow, agonising wave, the humiliation intense. I couldn't believe I had put myself in this position *again*.

Then Mack said, his voice little more than a whisper, "You—you *love* me?"

Christ, what did he want? Blood?

"Yes! I love you!" I bit out. "Satisfied? You want me to say it again? I love you, Mack. *I love you*."

He glared at me. "You're saying that like you're repeating yourself but you never said it before."

"Wasn't it obvious?"

"No," he said, his belligerence matching mine now, "No, because you didn't *say* that. You just asked me to stay."

"I didn't just ask you, I *begged* you," I said tightly. "I begged you to give us a chance."

"That is not telling someone"—and here his voice grew hoarse— "that you *love* them."

I raked a hand through my hair. "Okay, fine, it's not *exactly* the same. But Jesus, Mack, I'd already put myself on the line by begging you to stay and *you said no*! What was I supposed to do? Humiliate myself even more?"

"I didn't say no, I—"

"Yes, you did," I interrupted. "You shook your head, Mack. I asked you to tell me what you were thinking and you didn't say anything. You gave me nothing at all. No reason to think your answer was anything but *no*. I don't—"

"And I'm sorry!" he cried, and his expression was distraught. "I fucked up, I know! But I really didn't want to be in love with you! The plan—my plan—was *not* to stay here."

I stared at him, struck dumb.

"I didn't want to be in love with you."

"Wait . . ." I said slowly, trying to parse his words. But it seemed he was on a roll now.

"I wasn't even sure that's what it was. But suddenly I wanted to be with you all the time and I'd never felt that way about any other person. I noticed all these little things about you, and they made me all so fucking sappy. Stupid shit, like how your hair curls at the nape of your neck and how you look when you're sleeping. And I was just—" He broke off.

"Just what?"

His gaze was bleak. "I was *happy*. Like I've never been before. I was—"

I whispered, "What?"

"Fucking terrified."

I stared at him. "Me too."

Strange how you can feel terrified and deliriously happy at the same time.

Slowly, carefully, I moved towards him. "I'm sorry for being a coward," I said. "I should have told you everything that night after the Sea Bell. I should have been braver about it. But me being an idiot doesn't change the fact that I do love you, Mack. And I really want you to stay."

"Nathan."

I was close enough to kiss him now, but in the end, it was him who kissed me, leaning forward to press his lips against mine. And god, I welcomed the warm slide of his tongue into my mouth, the hard length of his body against mine. His scent, warm and familiar. I'd missed that. Missed him. Holding him like this set everything in my world the right way up again.

When we broke apart, I said breathlessly, "So, will you stay now?"

"Yeah," he whispered.

I swallowed, hard. "For how long?"

"How long do you want me here?"

"Forever." I touched his cheek. "But we can take it at your pace. Whatever you're comfortable with. Just—no secrets, yeah? From now on, you tell me what's on your mind."

He smiled. "That goes two ways. I'll promise if you will."

"Okay. I promise."

He sighed then, resting his forehead against mine. Closed his eyes. "Will you take me to bed now?"

"Yes," I breathed. "Let's go to bed."

"And no more nights apart?"

"No," I agreed.

I planned to hold onto him from now on.

All night and every night.

EPILOGUE

Mack – One year later

I've never much liked Christmas but this year is different.

This year, I'm spending Christmas with Nathan. Well, Nathan and Rosie. And Dad and Lorraine.

The family.

I'm not sure that's how I think of them yet. Maybe I'll never really think of them that way. Except Nathan.

When I get to the café, Dad's balancing on a stepladder, putting up the last of the Christmas garlands, Michael Bublé's playing on the stereo—you can't beat a bit of Micky Bubbles at Christmas—and Rosie's behind the counter, wrapping up the sandwich-filling tubs for the day.

"Hi, son." Dad glances down at me, smiling.

Still not used to that. At some point over the last few months—after our big talk—he began to relax round me a bit more. Stopped looking so goddamned guilty all the time. I smile back, hoping I seem as relaxed to him. I still don't feel completely comfortable around Dad, but it's getting easier all the time.

"Where's Nathan?" I ask.

"Through the back, getting ready for you coming."

I slip behind the counter, where Rosie's pottering. She's pink-cheeked and whistling, a picture of good health. That's not the whole story, of course. She still has to be careful—always will—with her diet and her meds, but she doesn't let that stop her doing anything. She's even started a band with some of her school friends. They're pretty awful right now, but who knows where they might end up. She's fierce, my sister.

"Hey you." I tousle her hair. She's had it shaved on one side and dyed the ends purple. Derek just about had a fuckin' canary when he clocked it—I nearly pissed myself laughing when I saw his face.

"Hey you back." She grins. "So, where are you and Nathan off to then?"

"Out," I say.

She raises a brow. "Like on a *date*?"

"Like on a date," I confirm.

She grins. "More than a drink in The Bell?"

"Yup." I confirm, but don't give her anything more. Tonight's a surprise for Nathan. He doesn't know what I've got planned. Dad and Lorraine know—I wanted to check they were okay with it first—but they're sworn to secrecy.

Lorraine cried, of course. but then Lorraine always cries at times like this. Dad was a wee bit freaked to start with, but he soon came round. He loves Nathan. And Rosie will be delighted—of that much I'm sure.

I head into the kitchen to find Nathan removing his apron. It's half over his head and his T-shirt's riding up, exposing a delicious slice of his naked chest and stomach. I'm reminded of that first night I met him when he got all tangled up and flustered. He didn't seem to realise how much I fancied him. That's so typical of him.

I cross the floor, sliding my arms round his waist and he starts laughing. Somehow we get him disentangled from the apron and it lands on the floor as my lips meet his.

God, I love kissing Nathan.

I didn't like kissing before I met him. Difficult to forget how close you're letting someone get to you when their face is shoved up against your own and you're sharing breath and spit.

It's different with Nathan, though. Being close to him like that. I remember the first time he showed me what it could be like. He'd moved in slowly as I'd stared into his eyes, fascinated by all the shades of pale green, gold and brown. I'd been thinking how amazing it was to draw his scent into my lungs and just hold it there as our lips pressed together and our tongues tangled.

I'd never felt that way before.

I guess that was one of my first clues.

Nathan leans back in our embrace and considers me. "So," he says. "Where are you taking me?"

"Guess."

"The Orchid," he says, naming our favourite Thai place.

"Nope."

"Gennaro's?"

"Nope."

He laughs. "Tell me then."

"The Hope and Anchor."

It's the only Michelin-starred place for miles around and very expensive. But I want tonight to be memorable.

"Oh?" he says, eyes going wide. "Fancy! What are we celebrating?"

I think of the box in my pocket and what it contains. What I'll be asking him later. But for now, I just smile.

"Us," I say. "We're celebrating us."

PROOF

Explore more of the *Porthkennack* universe:
riptidepublishing.com/titles/universe/porthkennack

a PORTHKENNACK CONTEMPORARY

Wake Up Call
JL Merrow

Foxglove Copse
Alex Beecroft

Broke Deep
Charlie Cochrane

Junkyard Heart
Garrett Leigh

House of Cards
Garrett Leigh

a PORTHKENNACK HISTORICAL

A Gathering Storm
Joanna Chambers

Count the Shells
Charlie Cochrane

PROOF

Dear Reader,

Thank you for reading Joanna Chambers's *Tribute Act*!

We know your time is precious and you have many, many entertainment options, so it means a lot that you've chosen to spend your time reading. We really hope you enjoyed it.

We'd be honored if you'd consider posting a review—good or bad—on sites like **Amazon, Barnes & Noble, Kobo, Goodreads, Twitter, Facebook, Tumblr,** and your blog or website. We'd also be honored if you told your friends and family about this book. Word of mouth is a book's lifeblood!

For more information on upcoming releases, author interviews, blog tours, contests, giveaways, and more, please sign up for our weekly, spam-free newsletter and visit us around the web:

Newsletter: tinyurl.com/RiptideSignup
Twitter: twitter.com/RiptideBooks
Facebook: facebook.com/RiptidePublishing
Goodreads: tinyurl.com/RiptideOnGoodreads
Tumblr: riptidepublishing.tumblr.com

Thank you so much for Reading the Rainbow!

RiptidePublishing.com

PROOF

ACKNOWLEDGEMENTS

Huge thanks to my wonderful beta readers on this book: Susana, Con, Laura Adriana, Elizabeth, Alyson, Darla and Liv. Your insights were invaluable! xoxo

Also by
Joanna Chambers

A Gathering Storm (*a Porthkennack novel*)

The Enlightenment Series
Provoked
Beguiled
Enlightened
Seasons Pass
Unnatural

Enemies Like You, with Annika Martin
The Dream Alchemist
Unforgivable
The Lady's Secret

Novellas and Short Stories
Humbug
Rest and Be Thankful
Introducing Mr. Winterbourne (in the *Another Place in Time*
anthology)
Mr. Perfect's Christmas (in the *Wish Come True* anthology)

PROOF

ABOUT
THE AUTHOR

Joanna Chambers always wanted to write. In between studying, finding a proper grown-up job, getting married, and having kids, she spent many hours staring at blank sheets of paper and chewing pens. That changed when she rediscovered her love of romance and found her muse. Joanna's muse likes red wine and coffee and won't let Joanna clean the house or watch television.

You can find Joanna at joannachambers.com, friend her on Facebook at facebook.com/joanna.chambers.58, follow her on Twitter @ChambersJoanna, and connect with her on Goodreads atgoodreads.com/author/show/3080608.Joanna_Chambers.

PROOF

Enjoy more stories like
Tribute Act
at RiptidePublishing.com!

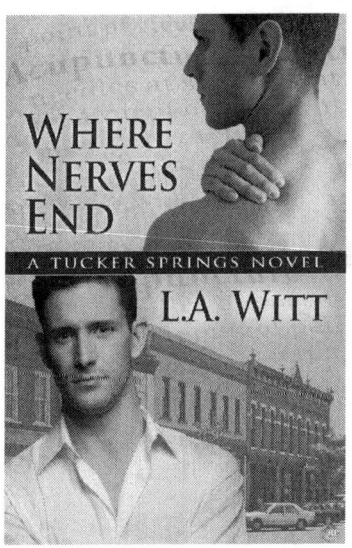

Where Nerves End
ISBN: 978-1-62649-168-7

A Fortunate Blizzard
ISBN: 978-1-62649-340-7

Earn Bonus Bucks!
Earn 1 Bonus Buck for each dollar you spend. Find out how at
RiptidePublishing.com/news/bonus-bucks.

Win Free Ebooks for a Year!
Pre-order coming soon titles directly through our site and you'll
receive one entry into a drawing for a chance to win free books for
a year! Get the details at RiptidePublishing.com/contests.

PROOF

78489907R00119

Made in the USA
Columbia, SC
17 October 2017